STAY OUT of the BASEMENT

GOOSEBUMPS®
HALL OF HORRORS

#1 CLAWS!

#2 NIGHT OF THE GIANT EVERYTHING

#3 SPECIAL EDITION: THE FIVE MASKS OF DR. SCREEM

#4 WHY I QUIT ZOMBIE SCHOOL

#5 DON'T SCREAM!

#6 THE BIRTHDAY PARTY OF NO RETURN

GOOSEBUMPS® WANTED:
THE HAUNTED MASK

GOOSEBUMPS®
MOST WANTED

#1 PLANET OF THE LAWN GNOMES

#2 SON OF SLAPPY

#3 HOW I MET MY MONSTER

#4 FRANKENSTEIN'S DOG

#5 DR. MANIAC WILL SEE YOU NOW

#6 CREATURE TEACHER: FINAL EXAM

#7 A NIGHTMARE ON CLOWN STREET

SPECIAL EDITION #1 ZOMBIE HALLOWEEN

SPECIAL EDITION #2 THE 12 SCREAMS OF CHRISTMAS

SPECIAL EDITION #3 TRICK OR TRAP

Goosebumps®

STAY OUT of the BASEMENT

R.L. STINE

SCHOLASTIC INC.

NEW YORK TORONTO LONDON AUCKLAND
SYDNEY MEXICO CITY NEW DELHI HONG KONG

ISBN 978-0-545-29838-4

12 11 10 9   16/0

Printed in the U.S.A.   40
First printing, November 2011

"Behind the Screams" bonus material by Gabrielle S. Balkan

1

"Hey, Dad — catch!"

Casey tossed the Frisbee across the smooth, green lawn. Casey's dad made a face, squinting into the sun. The Frisbee hit the ground and skipped a few times before landing under the hedge at the back of the house.

"Not today. I'm busy," Dr. Brewer said, and abruptly turned and loped into the house. The screen door slammed behind him.

Casey brushed his straight blond hair back off his forehead. "What's *his* problem?" he called to Margaret, his sister, who had watched the whole scene from the side of the redwood garage.

"You know," Margaret said quietly. She wiped her hands on the legs of her jeans and held them both up, inviting a toss. "I'll play Frisbee with you for a little while," she said.

"Okay," Casey said without enthusiasm. He walked slowly over to retrieve the Frisbee from under the hedge.

1

Margaret moved closer. She felt sorry for Casey. He and their dad were really close, always playing ball or Frisbee or video games together. But Dr. Brewer didn't seem to have time for that anymore.

Jumping up to catch the Frisbee, Margaret realized she felt sorry for herself, too. Dad hadn't been the same to her, either. In fact, he spent so much time down in the basement, he barely said a word to her.

He doesn't even call me Princess anymore, Margaret thought. It was a nickname she hated. But at least it was a nickname, a sign of closeness.

She tossed the red Frisbee back. A bad toss. Casey chased after it, but it sailed away from him. Margaret looked up to the golden hills beyond their backyard.

California, she thought.

It's so weird out here. Here it is, the middle of winter, and there isn't a cloud in the sky, and Casey and I are out in jeans and T-shirts as if it were the middle of summer.

She made a diving catch for a wild toss, rolling over on the manicured lawn and raising the Frisbee above her head triumphantly.

"Show-off," Casey muttered, unimpressed.

"You're the hot dog in the family," Margaret called.

"Well, you're a dork."

"Hey, Casey — you want me to play with you or not?"

He shrugged.

Everyone was so edgy these days, Margaret realized.

It was easy to figure out why.

She made a high toss. The Frisbee sailed over Casey's head. "*You* chase it!" he cried angrily, putting his hands on his hips.

"No, *you*!" she cried.

"You!"

"Casey — you're eleven years old. Don't act like a two-year-old," she snapped.

"Well, you act like a *one*-year old," was his reply as he grudgingly went after the Frisbee.

It was all Dad's fault, Margaret realized. Things had been so tense ever since he started working at home. Down in the basement with his plants and weird machines. He hardly ever came up for air.

And when he did, he wouldn't even catch a Frisbee.

Or spend two minutes with either of them.

Mom has noticed it, too, Margaret thought, running full-out and making another grandstand catch just before colliding with the side of the garage.

Having Dad home has made Mom really tense. She pretends everything is fine. But I can tell she's worried about him.

"Lucky catch, Fatso!" Casey called.

Margaret hated the name Fatso even more than she hated Princess. People in her family jokingly called her Fatso because she was so thin, like her father. She also was tall like him, but she had her mother's straight brown hair, brown eyes, and dark coloring.

"Don't call me that." She heaved the red disc at him. He caught it at his knees and flipped it back to her.

They tossed it back and forth without saying much for another ten or fifteen minutes. "I'm getting hot," Margaret said, shielding her eyes from the afternoon sun with her hand. "Let's go in."

Casey tossed the Frisbee against the garage wall. It dropped onto the grass. He came trotting over to her. "Dad always plays longer," he said peevishly. "And he throws better. You throw like a girl."

"Give me a break," Margaret groaned, giving him a playful shove as she jogged to the back door. "You throw like a chimpanzee."

"How come Dad got fired?" he asked.

She blinked. And stopped running. The question had caught her by surprise. "Huh?"

His pale, freckled face turned serious. "You know. I mean, why?" he asked, obviously uncomfortable.

She and Casey had never discussed this in the four weeks since Dad had been home. Which was unusual since they were pretty close, being only a year apart.

"I mean, we came all the way out here so he could work at PolyTech, right?" Casey asked.

"Yeah. Well . . . he got fired," Margaret said, half-whispering in case their dad might be able to hear.

"But why? Did he blow up the lab or something?" Casey grinned. The idea of their dad blowing up a huge campus science lab appealed to him.

"No, he didn't blow anything up," Margaret said, tugging at a strand of dark hair. "Botanists work with plants, you know. They don't get much of a chance to blow things up."

They both laughed.

Casey followed her into the narrow strip of shade cast by the low ranch-style house.

"I'm not sure exactly what happened," Margaret continued, still half whispering. "But I overheard Dad on the phone. I think he was talking to Mr. Martinez. His department head. Remember? The quiet little man who came to dinner that night the barbecue grill caught fire?"

Casey nodded. "Martinez fired Dad?"

"Probably," Margaret whispered. "From what I overhead, it had something to do with the plants Dad was growing, some experiments that had gone wrong or something."

5

"But Dad's real smart," Casey insisted, as if Margaret were arguing with him. "If his experiments went wrong, he'd know how to fix them."

Margaret shrugged. "That's all I know," she said. "Come on, Casey. Let's go inside. I'm dying of thirst!" She stuck her tongue out and moaned, demonstrating her dire need of liquid.

"You're gross," Casey said. He pulled open the screen door, then dodged in front of her so he could get inside first.

"Who's gross?" Mrs. Brewer asked from the sink. She turned to greet the two of them. "Don't answer that."

Mom looks very tired today, Margaret thought, noticing the crisscross of fine lines at the corners of her mother's eyes and the first strands of gray in her mother's shoulder-length brown hair. "I hate this job," Mrs. Brewer said, turning back to the sink.

"What are you doing?" Casey asked, pulling open the refrigerator and removing a box of juice.

"I'm deveining shrimp."

"Yuck!" Margaret exclaimed.

"Thanks for the support," Mrs. Brewer said dryly. The phone rang. Wiping her shrimpy hands with a dish towel, she hurried across the room to pick up the phone.

Margaret got a box of juice from the fridge, popped the straw into the top, and followed

6

Casey into the front hallway. The basement door, usually shut tight when Dr. Brewer was working down there, was slightly ajar.

Casey started to close it, then stopped. "Let's go down and see what Dad is doing," he suggested.

Margaret sucked the last drops of juice through the straw and squeezed the empty box flat in her hand. "Okay."

She knew they probably shouldn't disturb their father, but her curiosity got the better of her. He had been working down there for four weeks now. All kinds of interesting equipment, lights, and plants had been delivered. Most days he spent at least eight or nine hours down there, doing whatever it was he was doing. And he hadn't shown it to them once.

"Yeah. Let's go," Margaret said. It was *their* house, too, after all.

Besides, maybe their dad was just waiting for them to show some interest. Maybe he was hurt that they hadn't bothered to come downstairs in all this time.

She pulled the door open the rest of the way, and they stepped onto the narrow stairway. "Hey, Dad —" Casey called excitedly. "Dad — can we see?"

They were halfway down when their father appeared at the foot of the stairs. He glared up at them angrily, his skin strangely green under the

7

fluorescent light fixture. He was holding his right hand, drops of red blood falling onto his white lab coat.

"*Stay out of the basement!*" he bellowed, in a voice they'd never heard before.

Both kids shrank back, surprised to hear their father scream like that. He was usually so mild and soft-spoken.

"*Stay out of the basement,*" he repeated, holding his bleeding hand. "Don't *ever* come down here — I'm warning you."

"Okay. All packed," Mrs. Brewer said, dropping her suitcases with a thud in the front hallway. She poked her head into the living room, where the TV was blaring. "Do you think you could stop the movie for one minute to say good-bye to your mother?"

Casey pushed a button on the remote control, and the screen went blank. He and Margaret obediently walked to the hallway to give their mother hugs.

Margaret's friend Diane Manning, who lived just around the corner, followed them into the hallway. "How long are you going to be gone, Mrs. Brewer?" she asked, her eyes on the two bulging suitcases.

"I don't know," Mrs. Brewer replied fretfully. "My sister went into the hospital in Tucson this morning. I guess I'll have to stay until she's able to go home."

"Well, I'll be glad to babysit for Casey and Margaret while you're away," Diane joked.

"Give me a break," Margaret said, rolling her eyes. "I'm older than you are, Diane."

"And I'm smarter than both of you," Casey added with typical modesty.

"I'm not worried about you kids," Mrs. Brewer said, glancing nervously at her watch. "I'm worried about your father."

"Don't worry," Margaret told her seriously. "We'll take good care of him."

"Just make sure that he eats something once in a while," Mrs. Brewer said. "He's so obsessed with his work, he doesn't remember to eat unless you tell him."

It's going to be really lonely around here without Mom, Margaret thought. *Dad hardly ever comes up from the basement.*

It had been two weeks since he'd yelled at Casey and her to stay out of the basement. They had been tiptoeing around ever since, afraid to get him angry again. But in the past two weeks, he had barely spoken to them, except for the occasional "good morning" and "good night."

"Don't worry about anything, Mom," she said, forcing a smile. "Just take good care of Aunt Eleanor."

"I'll call as soon as I get to Tucson," Mrs. Brewer said, nervously lowering her eyes to her watch again. She took three long strides to the

basement door, then shouted down, "Michael —
time to take me to the airport!"

After a long wait, Dr. Brewer called up a reply.
Then Mrs. Brewer turned back to the kids.
"Think he'll even notice I'm gone?" she asked in
a loud whisper. She meant it to be a light remark,
but her eyes revealed some sadness.

A few seconds later, they heard footsteps
on the basement stairs, and their dad appeared.
He pulled off his stained lab coat, revealing
tan slacks and a bright yellow T-shirt, and tossed
the lab coat onto the banister. Even though it
was two weeks later, his right hand, the hand
that had been bleeding, was still heavily
bandaged.

"Ready?" he asked his wife.

Mrs. Brewer sighed. "I guess." She gave
Margaret and Casey a helpless look, then moved
quickly to give them each one last hug.

"Let's go, then," Dr. Brewer said impatiently.
He picked up the two bags and groaned. "Wow.
How long are you planning to stay? A year?"
Then he headed out the front door with them, not
waiting for an answer.

"Bye, Mrs. Brewer," Diane said, waving. "Have
a good trip."

"How can she have a good trip?" Casey asked
sharply. "Her sister's in the hospital."

"You know what I mean," Diane replied, tossing back her long red hair and rolling her eyes.

11

They watched the station wagon roll down the driveway, then returned to the living room. Casey picked up the remote control and started the movie.

Diane sprawled on the couch and picked up the bag of potato chips she'd been eating.

"Who picked this movie?" Diane asked, crinkling the foil bag noisily.

"I did," Casey said. "It's neat." He had pulled a couch cushion down to the living room carpet and was lying on it.

Margaret was sitting cross-legged on the floor, her back against the base of an armchair, still thinking about her mother and her aunt Eleanor. "It's neat if you like to see a lot of people blown up and their guts flying all over," she said, making a face for Diane's benefit.

"Yeah. It's neat," Casey said, not taking his eyes off the glowing TV screen.

"I've got so much homework. I don't know why I'm sitting here," Diane said, reaching her hand into the potato chip bag.

"Me, too." Margaret sighed. "I guess I'll do it after dinner. Do you have the math assignment? I think I left my math book at school."

"Sshhh!" Casey hissed, kicking a sneakered foot in Margaret's direction. "This is a good part."

"You've seen this movie before?" Diane shrieked.

"Twice," Casey admitted. He ducked, and the sofa pillow Diane threw sailed over his head.

"It's a pretty afternoon," Margaret said, stretching her arms above her head. "Maybe we should go outside. You know. Ride our bikes or something."

"You think you're still back in Michigan? It's *always* a pretty afternoon here," Diane said, chewing loudly. "I don't even notice it anymore."

"Maybe we should do the math assignment together," Margaret suggested hopefully. Diane was much better in math than she was.

Diane shrugged. "Yeah. Maybe." She crinkled up the bag and set it on the floor. "Your dad looked kind of nervous, you know?"

"Huh? What do you mean?"

"Just nervous," Diane said. "How's he doing?"

"Sshhh," Casey insisted, picking up the potato chip bag and tossing it at Diane.

"You know. Being laid off and all."

"I guess he's okay," Margaret said wistfully. "I don't know, really. He spends all his time down in the basement with his experiments."

"Experiments? Hey — let's go take a look." Tossing her hair back behind her shoulders, Diane jumped up from the chrome and white leather couch.

Diane was a science freak. Math and science. The two subjects Margaret hated.

She *should have been in the Brewer family*, Margaret thought with a trace of bitterness. *Maybe Dad would pay some attention to her since she's into the same things he is.*

"Come on —" Diane urged, bending over to pull Margaret up from the floor. "He's a botanist, right? What's he doing down there?"

"It's complicated," Margaret said, shouting over the explosions and gunfire on the TV. "He tried to explain it to me once. But —" Margaret allowed Diane to pull her to her feet.

"Shut up!" Casey yelled, staring at the movie, the colors from the TV screen reflecting over his clothes.

"Is he building a Frankenstein monster or something?" Diane demanded. "Or some kind of RoboCop? Wouldn't that be cool?"

"Shut up!" Casey repeated shrilly as the movie's hero bounded across the screen.

"He's got all these machines and plants down there," Margaret said uncomfortably. "But he doesn't want us to go down there."

"Huh? It's, like, top secret?" Diane's emerald green eyes lit up with excitement. "Come on. We'll just take a peek."

"No, I don't think so," Margaret told her. She couldn't forget the angry look on her father's face two weeks before when she and Casey had tried to pay a visit. Or the way he had screamed at them never to come down to the basement.

14

"Come on. I dare you," Diane challenged. "Are you chicken?"

"I'm not afraid," Margaret insisted shrilly. Diane was always daring her to do things she didn't want to do. *Why is it so important for Diane to think she's so much braver than everyone else?* Margaret wondered.

"Chicken," Diane repeated. Tossing her mane of red hair behind her shoulder, she strode quickly toward the basement door.

"Diane — stop!" Margaret cried, following after her.

"Hey, wait!" Casey cried, clicking off the movie. "Are we going downstairs? Wait for me!" He climbed quickly to his feet and enthusiastically hurried to join them at the basement door.

"We can't —" Margaret started, but Diane clamped a hand over her mouth.

"We'll take a quick peek," Diane insisted. "We'll just look. We won't touch anything. And then we'll come right back upstairs."

"Okay. I'll go first," Casey said, grabbing for the doorknob.

"Why do you want to do this?" Margaret asked her friend. "Why are you so eager to go down there?"

Diane shrugged. "It beats doing our math," she replied, grinning.

Margaret sighed, defeated. "Okay, let's go. But remember — just looking, no touching."

Casey pulled open the door and led the way onto the stairway. Stepping onto the landing, they were immediately engulfed in hot, steamy air. They could hear the buzz and hum of electronic machinery. And off to the right, they could see the glare of the bright white lights from Dr. Brewer's workroom.

This is kind of fun, Margaret thought as the three of them made their way down the linoleum-covered stairway.

It's an adventure.

There's no harm in taking a peek.

So why was her heart pounding? Why did she have this sudden tingle of fear?

"Yuck! It's so hot in here!"

As they stepped away from the stairs, the air became unbearably hot and thick.

Margaret gasped. The sudden change in temperature was suffocating.

"It's so moist," Diane said. "Good for your hair and skin."

"We studied the rain forest in school," Casey said. "Maybe Dad's building a rain forest."

"Maybe," Margaret said uncertainly.

Why did she feel so strange? Was it just because they were invading their father's domain? Doing something he had told them not to do?

She held back, gazing in both directions. The basement was divided into two large, rectangular rooms. To the left, an unfinished rec room stood in darkness. She could barely make out the outlines of the Ping-Pong table in the center of the room.

The workroom to the right was brightly lit, so bright they had to blink and wait for their eyes to adjust. Beams of white light poured down from large halogen lamps on tracks in the ceiling.

"Wow! Look!" Casey cried, his eyes wide as he stepped excitedly toward the light.

Reaching up toward the lights were tall, shiny plants, dozens of them, thick-stalked and broad-leafed, planted close together in an enormous, low trough of dark soil.

"It's like a jungle!" Margaret exclaimed, following Casey into the white glare.

The plants, in fact, resembled jungle plants — leafy vines and tall, treelike plants with long, slender tendrils, fragile-looking ferns, plants with gnarled, cream-colored roots poking up like bony knees from the soil.

"It's like a swamp or something," Diane said. "Did your father really grow these things in just five or six weeks?"

"Yeah. I'm pretty sure," Margaret replied, staring at the enormous red tomatoes on a slender yellow stalk.

"Ooh. Feel this one," Diane said.

Margaret glanced over to find her friend rubbing her hand over a large, flat leaf the shape of a teardrop. "Diane — we shouldn't touch —"

"I know, I know," Diane said, not letting go of the leaf. "But just rub your hand on it."

Margaret reluctantly obeyed. "It doesn't feel like a leaf," she said as Diane moved over to examine a large fern. "It's so smooth. Like glass."

The three of them stood under the bright white lights, examining the plants for several minutes, touching the thick stalks, running their hands over the smooth, warm leaves, surprised by the enormous size of the fruits some of the plants had produced.

"It's too hot down here," Casey complained. He pulled his T-shirt off over his head and dropped it onto the floor.

"What a bod!" Diane teased him.

He stuck out his tongue at her. Then his pale blue eyes grew wide and he seemed to freeze in surprise. "Hey!"

"Casey — what's the matter?" Margaret asked, hurrying over to him.

"This one —" He pointed to a tall, treelike plant. "It's *breathing*!"

Diane laughed.

But Margaret heard it, too. She grabbed Casey's bare shoulder and listened. Yes. She could hear breathing sounds, and they seemed to be coming from the tall, leafy tree.

"What's your problem?" Diane asked, seeing the amazed expressions on Casey's and Margaret's faces.

"Casey's right," Margaret said softly, listening to the steady, rhythmic sound. "You can hear it breathing."

Diane rolled her eyes. "Maybe it has a cold. Maybe its vine is stuffed up." She laughed at her own joke, but her two companions didn't join in. "I don't hear it." She moved closer.

All three of them listened.

Silence.

"It — stopped," Margaret said.

"Stop it, you two," Diane scolded. "You're not going to scare me."

"No. Really," Margaret protested.

"Hey — look at this!" Casey had already moved on to something else. He was standing in front of a tall glass case that stood on the other side of the plants. It looked a little like a phone booth, with a shelf inside about shoulder-high, and dozens of wires attached to the back and sides.

Margaret's eyes followed the wires to a similar glass booth a few feet away. Some kind of electrical generator stood between the two booths and appeared to be connected to both of them.

"What could that be?" Diane asked, hurrying over to Casey.

"Don't touch it," Margaret warned, giving the breathing plant one final glance, then joining the others.

But Casey reached out to the glass door on the

front of the booth. "I just want to see if this opens," he said.

He grabbed the glass — and his eyes went wide with shock.

His entire body began to shake and vibrate. His head jerked wildly from side to side. His eyes rolled up in his head.

"Oh, help!" he managed to cry, his body vibrating and shaking harder and faster. "Help me! I — can't stop!"

"Help me!"

Casey's whole body shook as if an electrical current were charging through him. His head jerked on his shoulders, and his eyes looked wild and dazed.

"Please!"

Margaret and Diane stared in openmouthed horror. Margaret was the first to move. She lunged at Casey and reached out to try to pull him away from the glass.

"Margaret — don't!" Diane screamed. "Don't touch him!"

"But we have to do something!" Margaret cried.

It took both girls a while to realize that Casey had stopped shaking. And was laughing.

"Casey?" Margaret asked, staring at him, her terrified expression fading to astonishment.

He was leaning against the glass, his body still now, his mouth wrapped in a broad, mischievous grin.

"Gotcha!" he declared. And then began to laugh even harder, pointing at them and repeating the phrase through his triumphant laughter. "Gotcha! Gotcha!"

"That wasn't funny!" Margaret screamed.

"You were faking it?! I don't believe it!" Diane cried, her face as pale as the white lights above them, her lower lip trembling.

Both girls leaped onto Casey and pushed him to the floor. Margaret sat on top of him while Diane held his shoulders down.

"Gotcha! Gotcha!" he continued, stopping only when Margaret tickled his stomach so hard he couldn't talk.

"You rat!" Diane cried. "You little rat!"

The free-for-all was brought to a sudden halt by a low moan from across the room. All three kids raised their heads and stared in the direction of the sound.

The large basement was silent now except for their heavy breathing.

"What was that?" Diane whispered.

They listened.

Another low moan, a mournful sound, muffled, like air through a saxophone.

The tendrils of a treelike plant suddenly drooped, like snakes lowering themselves to the ground.

Another low, sad moan.

"It's — the plants!" Casey said, his expression

frightened now. He pushed his sister off him and climbed to his feet, brushing back his disheveled blond hair as he stood up.

"Plants don't cry and moan," Diane said, her eyes on the vast trough of plants that filled the room.

"These do," Margaret said.

Tendrils moved, like human arms shifting their position. They could hear breathing again, slow, steady breathing. Then a sigh, like air escaping.

"Let's get out of here," Casey said, edging toward the stairs.

"It's definitely creepy down here," Diane said, following him, her eyes remaining on the shifting, moaning plants.

"I'm sure Dad could explain it," Margaret said. Her words were calm, but her voice trembled, and she was backing out of the room, following Diane and Casey.

"Your dad is weird," Diane said, reaching the doorway.

"No, he isn't," Casey quickly insisted. "He's doing important work here."

A tall, treelike plant sighed and appeared to bend toward them, raising its tendrils as if beckoning to them, calling them back.

"Let's just get out of here!" Margaret exclaimed.

All three of them were out of breath by the time they ran up the stairs. Casey closed the door tightly, making sure it clicked shut.

"Weird," Diane repeated, playing nervously with a strand of her long red hair. "Definitely weird." It was her word of the day. But Margaret had to admit it was appropriate.

"Well, Dad warned us not to go down there," Margaret said, struggling to catch her breath. "I guess he knew it would look scary to us, and we wouldn't understand."

"I'm getting out of here," Diane said, only half-kidding. She stepped out of the screen door and turned back toward them. "Want to go over the math later?"

"Yeah. Sure," Margaret said, still thinking about the moaning, shifting plants. Some of them had seemed to be reaching out to them, crying out to them. But of course that was impossible.

"Later," Diane said, and headed at a trot down the drive.

Just as she disappeared, their father's dark blue station wagon turned the corner and started up the driveway. "Back from the airport," Margaret said. She turned from the door back to Casey a few yards behind her in the hallway. "Is the basement door closed?"

"Yeah," Casey replied, looking again to make sure. "No way Dad will know we —"

He stopped. His mouth dropped open, but no sound came out.

His face went pale.

"My T-shirt!" Casey exclaimed, slapping his bare chest. "I left it in the basement!"

"I've got to get it," Casey said. "Otherwise Dad'll know —"

"It's too late," Margaret interrupted, her eyes on the driveway. "He's already pulled up the drive."

"It'll only take a second," Casey insisted, his hand on the basement doorknob. "I'll run down and run right up."

"No!" Margaret stood tensely in the center of the narrow hallway, halfway between the front door and the basement door, her eyes toward the front. "He's parked. He's getting out of the car."

"But he'll know! He'll know!" Casey cried, his voice high and whiny.

"So?"

"Remember how mad he got last time?" Casey asked.

"Of course I remember," Margaret replied.

"But he's not going to kill us, Casey, just because we took a peek at his plants. He's —"

Margaret stopped. She moved closer to the screen door. "Hey, wait."

"What's going on?" Casey asked.

"Hurry!" Margaret turned and gestured with both hands. "Go! Get downstairs — fast! Mr. Henry from next door. He stopped Dad. They're talking about something in the drive."

With a loud cry, Casey flung open the basement door and disappeared. Margaret heard him clumping rapidly down the stairs. Then she heard his footsteps fade as he hurried into their father's workroom.

Hurry, Casey, she thought, standing guard at the front door, watching her father shielding his eyes from the sun with one hand as he talked with Mr. Henry.

Hurry.

You know Dad never talks for long with the neighbors.

Mr. Henry seemed to be doing all the talking. *Probably asking Dad some kind of favor*, Margaret thought. Mr. Henry wasn't handy at all, not like Dr. Brewer. And so he was always asking Margaret's dad to come over and help repair or install things.

Her father was nodding now, a tight smile on his face.

Hurry, Casey.

Get back up here. Where are you?

Still shielding his eyes, Dr. Brewer gave Mr. Henry a quick wave. Then both men spun around and began walking quickly toward their houses.

Hurry, Casey.

Casey — he's coming! Hurry! Margaret urged silently.

It doesn't take this long to pick your T-shirt up from the floor and run up the stairs.

It shouldn't *take this long.*

Her dad was on the front walk now. He spotted her in the doorway and waved.

Margaret returned the wave and looked back through the hallway to the basement door. "Casey — where are you?" she called aloud.

No reply.

No sound from the basement.

No sound at all.

Dr. Brewer had paused outside to inspect the rosebushes at the head of the front walk.

"Casey?" Margaret called.

Still no reply.

"Casey — hurry!"

Silence.

Her father was crouching down, doing something to the soil beneath the rosebushes.

With a feeling of dread weighing down her entire body, Margaret realized she had no choice.

She had to go downstairs and see what was keeping Casey.

Casey ran down the steps, leaning on the metal banister so that he could jump down two steps at a time. He landed hard on the cement basement floor and darted into the bright white light of the plant room.

Stopping at the entranceway, he waited for his eyes to adjust to the brighter-than-day light. He took a deep breath, inhaling the steamy air, and held it. It was so hot down there, so sticky. His back began to itch. The back of his neck tingled.

The jungle of plants stood as if at attention under the bright white lights.

He saw his T-shirt, lying crumpled on the floor a few feet from a tall, leafy tree. The tree seemed to lean toward the T-shirt, its long tendrils hanging down, loosely coiled on the soil around its trunk.

Casey took a timid step into the room.

Why am I so afraid? he wondered.

It's just a room filled with strange plants.

Why do I have the feeling that they're watching me? Waiting for me?

He scolded himself for being so afraid and took a few more steps toward the crumpled T-shirt on the floor.

Hey — wait.

The breathing.

There it was again.

Steady breathing. Not too loud. Not too soft, either.

Who could be breathing? *What* could be breathing?

Was it the big tree?

Casey stared at the shirt on the floor. So near. What was keeping him from grabbing it and running back upstairs? What was holding him back?

He took a step forward. Then another.

Was the breathing growing louder?

He jumped, startled by a sudden low moan from the big supply closet against the wall.

It sounded so human, as if someone were in there, moaning in pain.

"Casey — where are you?"

Margaret's voice sounded so far away, even though she was just at the head of the stairs.

"Okay so far," he called back to her. But his voice came out in a whisper. She probably couldn't hear him.

He took another step. Another.

The shirt was about three yards away.

A quick dash. A quick dive, and he'd have it.

Another low moan from the supply closet. A plant seemed to sigh. A tall fern suddenly dipped down, shifting its leaves.

"Casey?" He could hear his sister from upstairs, sounding very worried. "Casey — hurry!"

I'm trying, he thought. *I'm trying to hurry.*

What was holding him back?

Another low moan, this time from the other side of the room.

He took two more steps, then crouched, his arms straight out in front of him.

The shirt was almost within reach.

He heard a groaning sound, then more breathing.

He raised his eyes to the tall tree. The long, ropy tendrils had tensed. Stiffened. Or had he imagined it?

No.

They had been drooping loosely. Now they were taut. Ready.

Ready to grab him?

"Casey — hurry!" Margaret called, sounding even farther away.

He didn't answer. He was concentrating on the shirt. Just a few feet away. Just a few feet. Just a foot.

The plant groaned again.

"Casey? Casey?"

The leaves quivered all the way up the trunk.

Just a foot away. Almost in reach.

"Casey? Are you okay? *Answer* me!"

He grabbed the shirt.

Two snakelike tendrils swung out at him.

"Huh?" he cried out, paralyzed with fear. "What's happening?"

The tendrils wrapped themselves around his waist.

"Let go!" he cried, holding the T-shirt tightly in one hand, grabbing at the tendrils with the other.

The tendrils hung on and gently tightened around him.

Margaret? Casey tried calling, but no sound came out of his mouth. *Margaret?*

He jerked violently, then pulled straight ahead.

The tendrils held on.

They didn't squeeze him. They weren't trying to strangle him. Or pull him back.

But they didn't let go.

They felt warm and wet against his bare skin. Like animal arms. Not like a plant.

Help! He again tried to shout. He pulled once more, leaning forward, using all his strength.

No good.

He ducked low, hit the floor, tried to roll away.

The tendrils hung on.

The plant uttered a loud sigh.

"Let go!" Casey cried, finally finding his voice.

And then suddenly Margaret was standing beside him. He hadn't heard her come down the stairs. He hadn't seen her enter the room.

"Casey!" she cried. "What's —"

Her mouth dropped open and her eyes grew wide.

"It — won't let go!" he told her.

"No!" she screamed. And grabbed one of the tendrils with both hands. And tugged with all her strength.

The tendril resisted for only a moment, then went slack.

Casey uttered a joyful cry and spun away from the remaining tendril. Margaret dropped the tendril and grabbed Casey's hand and began running toward the stairs.

"Oh!"

They both stopped short at the bottom of the stairway.

Standing at the top was their father, glaring down at them, his hands balled into tight fists at his sides, his face rigid with anger.

"Dad — the plants!" Margaret cried.

He stared down at them, his eyes cold and angry, unblinking. He was silent.

"One grabbed Casey!" Margaret told him.

"I just went down to get my shirt," Casey said, his voice trembling.

They stared up at him expectantly, waiting for him to move, to unball his fists, to relax his hard expression, to speak. But he glared down at them for the longest time.

Finally, he said, "You're okay?"

"Yeah," they said in unison, both of them nodding.

Margaret realized she was still holding Casey's hand. She let go of it and reached for the banister.

"I'm very disappointed in you both," Dr. Brewer said in a low, flat voice, cool but not angry.

"Sorry," Margaret said. "We knew we shouldn't —"

"We didn't touch anything. Really!" Casey exclaimed.

"Very disappointed," their father repeated.

"Sorry, Dad."

Dr. Brewer motioned for them to come upstairs, then he stepped into the hallway.

"I thought he was going to yell at us," Casey whispered to Margaret as he followed her up the steps.

"That's not Dad's style," Margaret whispered back.

"He sure yelled at us the *last* time we started into the basement," Casey replied.

They followed their father into the kitchen. He motioned for them to sit down at the white Formica table, then dropped into a chair across from them.

His eyes went from one to the other, as if studying them, as if seeing them for the first time. His expression was totally flat, almost robotlike, revealing no emotion at all.

"Dad, what's with those plants?" Casey asked.

"What do you mean?" Dr. Brewer asked.

"They're — so weird," Casey said.

"I'll explain them to you someday," Dr. Brewer said flatly, still staring at the two of them.

"It looks very interesting," Margaret said, struggling to say the right thing.

Was their dad *trying* to make them feel uncomfortable? she wondered. If so, he was doing a good job of it.

This wasn't like him. Not at all. He was always a very direct person, Margaret thought. If he was angry, he said he was angry. If he was upset, he'd tell them he was upset.

So why was he acting so strange, so silent, so . . . cold?

"I asked you not to go in the basement," he said quietly, crossing his legs and leaning back so that the kitchen chair tilted back. "I thought I made it clear."

Margaret and Casey glanced at each other. Finally, Margaret said, "We won't do it again."

"But can't you take us down there and tell us what you're doing?" Casey asked. He still hadn't put the T-shirt on. He was holding it in a ball between his hands on the kitchen table.

"Yeah. We'd really like to understand it," Margaret added enthusiastically.

"Someday," their father said. He returned the chair to all four legs and then stood up. "We'll do it soon, okay?" He raised his arms above his head and stretched. "I've got to get back to work." He disappeared into the front hallway.

Casey raised his eyes to Margaret and shrugged. Their father reappeared, carrying the lab coat he had tossed over the front banister.

"Mom took off okay?" Margaret asked.

He nodded. "I guess." He pulled on the lab coat over his head.

"I hope Aunt Eleanor is okay," Margaret said.

Dr. Brewer's reply was muffled as he adjusted the lab coat and straightened the collar. "Later," he said. He disappeared into the hallway. They heard him shut the basement door behind him.

"I guess he's not going to ground us or anything for going down there," Margaret said, leaning against the table and resting her chin in her hands.

"I guess," Casey said. "He sure is acting . . . weird."

"Maybe he's upset because Mom is gone," Margaret said. She sat up and gave Casey a push. "Come on. Get up. I've got work to do."

"I can't believe that plant grabbed me," Casey said thoughtfully, not budging.

"You don't have to push," Casey griped, but he climbed to his feet and stepped out of Margaret's way. "I'm going to have bad dreams tonight," he said glumly.

"Just don't think about the basement,"

Margaret advised. *That's really lame advice,* she told herself. But what else could she say?

She went up to her room, thinking about how she missed her mother already. Then the scene in the basement with Casey trying to pull himself free of the enormous, twining plant tendrils played once again through her mind.

With a shudder, she grabbed her textbook and threw herself onto her stomach on the bed, prepared to read.

But the words on the page blurred as the moaning, breathing plants kept creeping back into her thoughts.

At least we're not being punished for going down there, she thought.

At least Dad didn't yell and frighten us this time.

And at least Dad has promised to take us downstairs with him soon and explain to us what he's working on down there.

That thought made Margaret feel a lot better.

She felt better until the next morning, when she awoke early and went downstairs to make some breakfast. To her surprise, her father was already at work, the basement door was shut tight, and a lock had been installed on the door.

The next Saturday afternoon, Margaret was up in her room, lying on top of the bed, talking to her mom on the phone. "I'm really sorry about Aunt Eleanor," she said, twisting the white phone cord around her wrist.

"The surgery didn't go as well as expected," her mother said, sounding very tired. "The doctors say she may have to have more surgery. But they have to build up her strength first."

"I guess this means you won't be coming home real soon," Margaret said sadly.

Mrs. Brewer laughed. "Don't tell me you actually miss me!"

"Well . . . yes," Margaret admitted. She raised her eyes to the bedroom window. Two sparrows had landed outside on the window ledge and were chattering excitedly, distracting Margaret, making it hard to hear her mother over the crackling line from Tucson.

"How's your father doing?" Mrs. Brewer asked. "I spoke to him last night, but he only grunted."

"He doesn't even grunt to us!" Margaret complained. She held her hand over her ear to drown out the chattering birds. "He hardly says a word."

"He's working really hard," Mrs. Brewer replied. In the background, Margaret could hear some kind of loudspeaker announcement. Her mother was calling from a pay phone at the hospital.

"He never comes out of the basement," Margaret complained, a little more bitterly than she had intended.

"Your father's experiments are very important to him," her mother said.

"More important than *we* are?" Margaret cried. She hated the whiny tone in her voice. She wished she hadn't started complaining about her dad over the phone. Her mother had enough to worry about at the hospital. Margaret knew she shouldn't make her feel even worse.

"Your dad has a lot to prove," Mrs. Brewer said. "To himself, and to others. I think he's working so hard because he wants to prove to Mr. Martinez and the others at the university that they were wrong to fire him. He wants to show them that they made a big mistake."

"But we used to see him more *before* he was home all the time!" Margaret complained.

She could hear her mother sigh impatiently. "Margaret, I'm trying to explain to you. You're old enough to understand."

"I'm sorry," Margaret said quickly. She decided to change the subject. "He's wearing a baseball cap all of a sudden."

"Who? Casey?"

"No, Mom," Margaret replied. "Dad. He's wearing a Dodgers cap. He never takes it off."

"Really?" Mrs. Brewer sounded very surprised.

Margaret laughed. "We told him he looks really dorky in it, but he refuses to take it off."

Mrs. Brewer laughed, too. "Uh-oh. I'm being called," she said. "Got to run. Take care, dear. I'll try to call back later."

A click, and she was gone.

Margaret stared up at the ceiling, watching shadows from trees in the front yard move back and forth. The sparrows had flown away, leaving silence behind.

Poor Mom, Margaret thought.

She's so worried about her sister, and I had to go and complain about Dad.

Why did I do that?

She sat up, listening to the silence. Casey was over at a friend's. Her dad was no doubt working in the basement, the door carefully locked behind him.

Maybe I'll give Diane a call, Margaret thought. She reached for the phone, then realized she was hungry. *Lunch first*, she decided. *Then Diane.*

She brushed her dark hair quickly, shaking her head at the mirror over her dressing table, then hurried downstairs.

To her surprise, her dad was in the kitchen. He was huddled over the sink, his back to her.

She started to call out to him but stopped. What was he doing?

43

Curious, she pressed against the wall, gazing at him through the doorway to the kitchen.

Dr. Brewer appeared to be eating something. With one hand, he was holding a bag on the counter beside the sink. As Margaret watched in surprise, he dipped his hand into the bag, pulled out a big handful of something, and shoved it into his mouth.

Margaret watched him chew hungrily, noisily, then pull out another handful from the bag and eat it greedily.

What on earth is he eating? she wondered. *He never eats with Casey and me. He always says he isn't hungry. But he sure is hungry now! He acts as if he's starving!*

She watched from the doorway as Dr. Brewer continued to grab handful after handful from the bag, gulping down his solitary meal. After a while, he crinkled up the bag and tossed it into the trash can under the sink. Then he wiped his hands off on the sides of his white lab coat.

Margaret quickly backed away from the door, tiptoed through the hall, and ducked into the living room. She held her breath as her father came into the hall, clearing his throat loudly.

The basement door closed behind him. She heard him carefully lock it.

When she was sure that he had gone downstairs, Margaret walked eagerly into the kitchen.

44

She had to know what her father had been eating so greedily, so hungrily.

She pulled open the sink cabinet, reached into the trash, and pulled out the crinkled-up bag.

Then she gasped aloud as her eyes ran over the label.

Her father, she saw, had been devouring *plant food.*

Margaret swallowed hard. Her mouth felt dry as cotton. She suddenly realized she was squeezing the side of the counter so tightly her hand ached.

Forcing herself to loosen her grip, she stared down at the half-empty plant food bag, which she had dropped onto the floor.

She felt sick. She couldn't get the disgusting picture out of her mind. How could her dad eat *mud*?

He didn't just eat it, she realized. He shoveled it into his mouth and gulped it down.

As if he *liked* it.

As if he *needed* it.

Eating the plant food had to be part of his experiments, Margaret told herself. But what *kind* of experiments? What was he trying to prove with those strange plants he was growing?

The stuff inside the bag smelled sour, like fertilizer. Margaret took a deep breath and held it.

46

She suddenly felt sick to her stomach. Staring at the bag, she couldn't help but imagine what the disgusting muck inside must taste like.

Ohh.

She nearly gagged.

How could her own father shove this horrid stuff into his mouth?

Still holding her breath, she grabbed the nearly empty bag, wadded it up, and tossed it back into the trash. She started to turn away from the counter when a hand grabbed her shoulder.

Margaret uttered a silent cry and spun around. "Casey!"

"I'm home," he said, grinning at her. "What's for lunch?"

Later, after making him a peanut butter sandwich, she told Casey what she had seen.

Casey laughed.

"It isn't funny," she said crossly. "Our own dad was eating dirt."

Casey laughed again. For some reason, it struck him as funny.

Margaret punched him hard on the shoulder, so hard that he dropped his sandwich. "Sorry," she said quickly, "but I don't see what you're laughing at. It's sick! There's something wrong with Dad. Something really wrong."

"Maybe he just had a craving for plant food," Casey cracked, still not taking her seriously. "You know. Like you get a craving for those honey-roasted peanuts."

"That's different," Margaret snapped. "Eating dirt is disgusting. Why won't you admit it?"

But before Casey could reply, Margaret continued, letting all of her unhappiness out at once. "Don't you see? Dad has changed. A lot. Even since Mom has been gone. He spends even more time in the basement —"

"That's because Mom isn't around," Casey interrupted.

"And he's so quiet all the time and so cold to us," Margaret continued, ignoring him. "He hardly says a word to us. He used to kid around all the time and ask us about our homework. He never says a human word. He never calls me Princess or Fatso the way he used to. He never —"

"You hate those names, Fatso," Casey said, giggling with a mouthful of peanut butter.

"I know," Margaret said impatiently. "That's just an example."

"So what are you trying to say?" Casey asked. "That Dad is out of his tree? That he's gone totally bananas?"

"I — I don't know," Margaret answered in frustration. "Watching him gulp down that disgusting plant food, I — I had this horrible thought that he's turning *into* a plant!"

Casey jumped up, causing his chair to scrape

back across the floor. He began staggering around the kitchen, zombielike, his eyes closed, his arms stretched out stiffly in front of him. "I am The Incredible Plant Man!" he declared, trying to make his voice sound bold and deep.

"Not funny," Margaret insisted, crossing her arms over her chest, refusing to be amused.

"Plant Man versus Weed Woman!" Casey declared, staggering toward Margaret.

"Not funny," she repeated.

He bumped into the counter, banging his knee. *"Ow!"*

"Serves you right," Margaret said.

"Plant Man kills!" he cried, and rushed at her. He ran right into her, using his head as a battering ram against her shoulder.

"Casey — will you stop it!" she screamed. "Give me a break!"

"Okay, okay." He backed off. "If you'll do me one favor."

"What favor?" Margaret asked, rolling her eyes.

"Make me another sandwich."

Monday afternoon after school, Margaret, Casey, and Diane were tossing a Frisbee back and forth in Diane's backyard. It was a warm, breezy day, the sky dotted with small, puffy white clouds.

Diane tossed the disc high. It sailed over Casey's head into the row of fragrant lemon trees that stretched from behind the clapboard garage. Casey went running after it and tripped over an in-ground sprinkler that poked up just an inch above the lawn.

Both girls laughed.

Casey, on the run, flung the Frisbee toward Margaret. She reached for it, but the breeze sent it sailing from her hand.

"What's it like to have a mad scientist for a dad?" Diane asked suddenly.

"What?" Margaret wasn't sure she'd heard right.

"Don't just stand there. Throw it!" Casey urged from beside the garage.

Margaret tossed the Frisbee high in the air in her brother's general direction. He liked to run and make diving catches.

"Just because he's doing strange experiments doesn't mean he's a mad scientist," Margaret said sharply.

"Strange is right," Diane said, her expression turning serious. "I had a nightmare last night about those gross plants in your basement. They were crying and reaching for me."

"Sorry," Margaret said sincerely. "I've had nightmares, too."

"Look out!" Casey cried. He tossed a low one that Diane caught around her ankles.

Mad scientist, Margaret thought. *Mad scientist. Mad scientist.*

The words kept repeating in her mind.

Mad scientists were only in the movies — right?

"My dad was talking about your dad the other night," Diane said, flipping the disc to Casey.

"You didn't tell him about — going down in the basement? Did you?" Margaret asked anxiously.

"No," Diane replied, shaking her head.

"Hey, are these lemons ripe?" Casey asked, pointing at one of the low trees.

"Why don't you suck one to find out?" Margaret snapped, annoyed that he kept interrupting.

"Why don't *you*?" he predictably shot back.

"My dad said that your dad was fired from PolyTech because his experiments got out of control, and he wouldn't stop them," Diane confided. She ran along the smooth, closely cropped grass, chasing down the Frisbee.

"What do you mean?" Margaret asked.

"The university told him he had to stop whatever it was he was doing, and he refused. He said he couldn't stop. At least that's what my dad heard from a guy who came into the salesroom."

Margaret hadn't heard this story. It made her feel bad, but she thought it was probably true.

"Something really bad happened in your dad's lab," Diane continued. "Someone got really hurt or killed or something."

"That's not true," Margaret insisted. "We would've heard if that happened."

"Yeah. Probably," Diane admitted. "But my dad said your dad was fired because he refused to stop his experiments."

"Well, that doesn't make him a mad scientist," Margaret said defensively. She suddenly felt she had to stick up for her father. She wasn't sure why.

"I'm just telling you what I heard," Diane said, brusquely tossing back her red hair. "You don't have to bite my head off."

They played for a few more minutes. Diane changed the subject and talked about some kids they knew who were eleven but were going out. Then they talked about school for a while.

"Time to go," Margaret called to Casey. He picked the Frisbee up from the lawn and came running over. "Call you later," Margaret told Diane, giving her a little wave. Then she and Casey began to jog home, cutting through familiar backyards.

"We need a lemon tree," Casey said as they slowed to a walk. "They're cool."

"Oh, yeah," Margaret replied sarcastically. "That's just what we need at our house. Another plant!"

As they stepped through the hedges into their backyard, they were both surprised to see their dad. He was standing at the rose trellis examining clusters of pink roses.

"Hey, Dad!" Casey called. "Catch!" He tossed the Frisbee to his father.

Dr. Brewer turned around a little too slowly. The Frisbee glanced off his head, knocking the Dodgers cap off. His mouth opened wide in surprise. He raised his hands to cover his head.

But it was too late.

Margaret and Casey both shrieked in surprise as they saw his head.

At first, Margaret thought her father's hair had turned green.

But then she clearly saw that it wasn't hair on his scalp.

His hair was gone. It had all fallen out.

In place of hair, Dr. Brewer had bright green leaves sprouting from his head.

"Kids — it's okay!" Dr. Brewer called. He bent down quickly, picked up the baseball cap, and replaced it on his head.

A crow flew low overhead, cawing loudly. Margaret raised her eyes to follow the bird, but the sight of the hideous leaves sprouting from her father's head wouldn't go away.

Her whole head began to itch as she imagined what it must feel like to have leaves uncurling from your scalp.

"It's okay. Really," Dr. Brewer repeated, hurrying over to them.

"But, Dad — your head," Casey stammered. He suddenly looked very pale.

Margaret felt sick. She kept swallowing hard, trying to ride out the waves of nausea.

"Come here, you two," their father said softly, putting an arm around each of their shoulders. "Let's sit down in the shade over there and have a talk. I spoke to your mom on the phone

54

this morning. She told me you're upset about my work."

"Your head — it's all green!" Casey repeated.

"I know," Dr. Brewer said, smiling. "That's why I put on the cap. I didn't want you two to worry."

He led them to the shade of the tall hedges that ran along the garage, and they sat down on the grass. "I guess you think your dad has gotten pretty weird, huh?"

He stared into Margaret's eyes. Feeling uncomfortable, she looked away.

Cawing frantically, the crow flew over again, heading in the other direction.

"Margaret, you haven't said a word," her father said, squeezing her hand tenderly between his. "What's wrong? What do you want to say to me?"

Margaret sighed and still avoided her father's glance. "Come on. Tell us. Why do you have leaves growing out of your head?" she asked bluntly.

"It's a side effect," he told her, continuing to hold her hand. "It's only temporary. It'll go away soon and my hair will grow back."

"But how did it happen?" Casey asked, staring at his father's Dodgers cap. A few green leaves poked out from under the brim.

"Maybe you two would feel better if I explained what I'm trying to do down in the basement," Dr. Brewer said, shifting his weight and leaning back on his hands. "I've been so wrapped up in my experiments, I haven't had much time to talk to you."

"You haven't had *any* time," Margaret corrected him.

"I'm sorry," he said, lowering his eyes. "I really am. But this work I'm doing is so exciting and so difficult."

"Did you discover a new kind of plant?" Casey asked, crossing his legs beneath him.

"No, I'm trying to *build* a new kind of plant," Dr. Brewer explained.

"Huh?" Casey exclaimed.

"Have you ever talked about DNA in school?" their father asked. They shook their heads. "Well, it's pretty complicated," he continued. Dr. Brewer thought for a moment. "Let me try and put it in simple terms," he said, fiddling with the bandage around his hand. "Let's say we took a person who had a very high IQ. You know. Real brain power."

"Like me," Casey interrupted.

"Casey, shut up," Margaret said edgily.

"A real brain. Like Casey," Dr. Brewer said agreeably. "And let's say we were able to isolate the molecule or gene or tiny part of a gene that enabled the person to have such high intelligence. And then let's say we were able to transmit it into other brains. And then this brain power

56

could be passed along from generation to generation. And lots of people would have high IQs. Do you understand?" He looked first at Casey, then at Margaret.

"Yeah. Kind of," Margaret said. "You take a good quality from one person and put it into other people. And then they have the good quality, too, and they pass it on to their children, and on and on."

"Very good," Dr. Brewer said, smiling for the first time in weeks. "That's what a lot of botanists do with plants. They try to take the fruit-bearing building block from one plant and put it into another. Create a new plant that will bear five times as much fruit, or five times as much grain, or vegetables."

"And that's what you're doing?" Casey asked.

"Not exactly," their father said, lowering his voice. "I'm doing something a little more unusual. I really don't want to go into detail now. But I'll tell you that what I'm trying to do is build a kind of plant that has never existed and *could* never exist. I'm trying to build a plant that's *part animal*."

Casey and Margaret stared at their father in surprise. Margaret was the first to speak. "You mean you're taking cells from an animal and putting them into a plant?"

He nodded. "I really don't want to say more. You two understand why this must be kept secret." He turned his eyes on Margaret, then Casey, studying their reactions.

"How do you do it?" Margaret asked, thinking hard about everything he had just told them. "How do you get these cells from the animals to the plant?"

"I'm trying to do it by breaking them down electronically," he answered. "I have two glass booths connected by a powerful electron generator. You may have seen them when you were snooping around down there." He made a sour face.

"Yeah. They look like phone booths," Casey said.

"One booth is a sender, and one is a receiver," he explained. "I'm trying to send the right DNA, the right building blocks, from one booth to the other. It's very delicate work."

"And have you done it?" Margaret asked.

"I've come very close," Dr. Brewer said, a pleased smile crossing his face. The smile lasted only a few seconds. Then, his expression thoughtful, he abruptly climbed to his feet. "Got to get back to work," he said quietly. "See you two later." He started walking across the lawn, taking long strides.

"But, Dad," Margaret called after him. She and Casey climbed to their feet, too. "Your head. The leaves. You didn't explain it," she said as she and her brother hurried to catch up to him.

Dr. Brewer shrugged. "Nothing to explain," he said curtly. "Just a side effect." He adjusted his Dodgers cap. "Don't worry about it. It's only temporary. Just a side effect."

Then he hurried into the house.

Casey seemed really pleased by their dad's explanation of what was going on in the basement. "Dad's doing really important work," he said, with unusual seriousness.

But as Margaret made her way into the house, she found herself troubled by what her dad had said. And even more troubled by what he *hadn't* said.

Margaret closed the door to her room and lay down on the bed to think about things. Her father hadn't really explained the leaves growing on his head. "Just a side effect" didn't explain much at all.

A side effect from what? What actually caused it? What made his hair fall out? When would his hair grow back?

It was obvious that he hadn't wanted to discuss it with them. He had certainly hurried back to his basement after telling them it was just a side effect.

A side effect.

It made Margaret feel sick every time she thought about it.

What must it feel like? Green leaves

pushing up from your pores, uncurling against your head.

Yuck. Thinking about it made her itch all over. She knew she'd have hideous dreams tonight.

She grabbed her pillow and hugged it over her stomach, wrapping her arms tightly around it.

There are lots of other questions Casey and I should have asked, she decided. *Like, why were the plants moaning down there? Why did some of them sound like they were breathing? Why did that plant grab Casey? What animal is Dad using?*

Lots of questions.

Not to mention the one Margaret wanted to ask most of all: *Why were you gulping down that disgusting plant food?*

But she couldn't ask that one. She couldn't let her dad know she'd been spying on him.

She and Casey hadn't really asked any of the questions they'd wanted answered. They were just so pleased that their father had decided to sit down and talk with them, even for a few minutes.

His explanation was really interesting, as far as it went, Margaret decided. And it was good to know that he was close to doing something truly amazing, something that would make him really famous.

But what about the rest of it?

A frightening thought entered her mind: Could he have been lying to them?

No, she quickly decided. *No. Dad wouldn't lie to us.*

There are just some questions he hasn't answered yet.

She was still thinking about all of these questions late that night — after dinner, after talking to Diane on the phone for an hour, after homework, after watching a little TV, after going to bed. And she was puzzling over them.

When she heard her father's soft footsteps coming up the carpeted stairs, she sat up in bed. A soft breeze fluttered the curtains across the room. She listened to her father's footsteps pass her room, heard him go into the bathroom, heard the water begin to run into the sink.

I've got to ask him, she decided.

Glancing at the clock, she saw that it was two thirty in the morning.

But she realized she was wide-awake.

I've got to ask him about the plant food.

Otherwise, it will drive me crazy. I'll think about it and think about it and think about it. Every time I see him, I'll picture him standing over the sink, shoving handful after handful into his mouth.

There's got to be a simple explanation, she told herself, climbing out of bed. *There's got to be a logical explanation.*

61

And I have to know it.

She padded softly down the hall, a sliver of light escaping through the bathroom door, which was slightly ajar. Water still ran into the sink.

She heard him cough, then heard him adjust the water.

I have to know the answer, she thought.

I'll just ask him point-blank.

She stepped into the narrow triangle of light and peered into the bathroom.

He was standing at the sink, leaning over it, his chest bare, his shirt tossed behind him on the floor. He had put the baseball cap on the closed toilet lid, and the leaves covering his head shone brightly under the bathroom light.

Margaret held her breath.

The leaves were so green, so thick.

He didn't notice her. He was concentrating on the bandage on his hand. Using a small scissors, he cut the bandage, then pulled it off.

The hand was still bleeding, Margaret saw.

Or was it?

What *was* that dripping from the cut on her father's hand?

Still holding her breath, she watched him wash it off carefully under the hot water. Then he examined it, his eyes narrowed in concentration.

After washing, the cut continued to bleed.

Margaret stared hard, trying to better focus her eyes.

It couldn't be blood — could it?

It couldn't be blood dripping into the sink.

It was bright green!

She gasped and started to run back to her room. The floor creaked under her footsteps.

"Who's there?" Dr. Brewer cried. "Margaret? Casey?"

He poked his head into the hallway as Margaret disappeared back into her room.

He saw me, she realized, leaping into bed.

He saw me — and now he's coming after me.

10

Margaret pulled the covers up to her chin. She realized she was trembling, her whole body shaking and chilled.

She held her breath and listened.

She could still hear water splashing into the bathroom sink.

But no footsteps.

He isn't coming after me, she told herself, letting out a long, silent sigh.

How could I have thought that? How could I have been so terrified — of my own father?

Terrified.

It was the first time the word had crossed her mind.

But sitting there in bed, trembling so violently, holding on to the covers so hard, listening for his approaching footsteps, Margaret realized that she was terrified.

Of her own father.

If only Mom were home, she thought.

Without thinking, she reached for the phone. She had the idea in her head to call her mother, wake her up, tell her to come home as fast as she could. Tell her something terrible was happening to Dad. That he was changing. That he was acting so weird. . . .

She glanced at the clock. Two forty-three.

No. She couldn't do that. Her poor mother was having such a terrible time in Tucson trying to care for her sister. Margaret couldn't frighten her like that.

Besides, what could she say? How could she explain to her mother how she had become terrified of her own father?

Mrs. Brewer would just tell her to calm down. That her father still loved her. That he would never harm her. That he was just caught up in his work.

Caught up . . .

He had leaves growing out of his head, he was eating dirt, and his blood was green.

Caught up . . .

She heard the water in the sink shut off. She heard the bathroom light being clicked off. Then she heard her father pad slowly to his room at the end of the hall.

Margaret relaxed a little, slid down in the bed, loosened her grip on the blankets. She closed her eyes and tried to clear her mind.

She tried counting sheep.

That never worked. She tried counting to one thousand. At 375, she sat up. Her head throbbed. Her mouth was as dry as cotton.

She decided to go downstairs and get a drink of cold water from the refrigerator.

I'm going to be a wreck tomorrow, she thought, making her way silently through the hall and down the stairs.

It is *tomorrow.*

What am I going to do? I've got to get to sleep.

The kitchen floor creaked beneath her bare feet. The refrigerator motor clicked on noisily, startling her.

Be cool, she told herself. *You've got to be cool.*

She had opened the refrigerator and was reaching for the water bottle when a hand grabbed her shoulder.

"Aii!" she cried out and dropped the open bottle onto the floor. Ice-cold water puddled around her feet. She leaped back, but her feet were soaked.

"Casey — you scared me!" she exclaimed. "What are you doing up?"

"What are *you* doing up?" he replied, half-asleep, his blond hair matted against his forehead.

"I couldn't sleep. Help me mop up this water."

"I didn't spill it," he said, backing away. "You mop it up."

"You *made* me spill it!" Margaret declared shrilly. She grabbed a roll of paper towels off the counter and handed him a wad of them. "Come on. Hurry."

They both got down on their knees and, by the light from the refrigerator, began mopping up the cold water.

"I just keep thinking about things," Casey said, tossing a soaking wad of paper towel onto the counter. "That's why I can't sleep."

"Me, too," Margaret said, frowning.

She started to say something else, but a sound from the hallway stopped her. It was a plaintive cry, a moan filled with sadness.

Margaret gasped and stopped dabbing at the water. "What was that?"

Casey's eyes filled with fear.

They heard it again, such a sad sound, like a plea, a mournful plea.

"It — it's coming from the basement," Margaret said.

"Do you think it's a plant?" Casey asked very quietly. "Do you think it's one of Dad's plants?"

Margaret didn't answer. She crouched on her knees, not moving, just listening.

Another moan, softer this time but just as mournful.

"I don't think Dad told us the truth," she told

Casey, staring into his eyes. He looked pale and frightened in the dim refrigerator light. "I don't think a tomato plant would make a sound like that."

Margaret climbed to her feet, collected the wet clumps of paper towel, and deposited them in the trash can under the sink. Then she closed the refrigerator door, covering the room in darkness.

Her hand on Casey's shoulder, she guided him out of the kitchen and through the hall. They stopped at the basement door and listened.

Silence now.

Casey tried the door. It was locked.

Another low moan, sounding very nearby now.

"It's so human," Casey whispered.

Margaret shuddered. What was going on down in the basement? What was *really* going on?

She led the way up the stairs and waited at her doorway until Casey was safely in his room. He gave her a wave, yawning silently, and closed the door behind him.

A few seconds later, Margaret was back in her bed, the covers pulled up to her chin despite the warmth of the night. Her mouth was still achingly dry, she realized. She had never managed to get a drink.

Somehow she drifted into a restless sleep.

Her alarm went off at seven thirty. She sat up and thought about school. Then she remembered there was no school for the next two days because of some kind of teachers' conference.

She turned off the clock radio, slumped back onto her pillow, and tried to go back to sleep. But she was awake now, thoughts of the night before pouring back into her mind, flooding her with the fear she had felt just a few hours earlier.

She stood up and stretched, and decided to go talk to her father, to confront him first thing, to ask all the questions she wanted to ask.

If I don't, he'll disappear down to the basement, and I'll sit around thinking these frightening thoughts all day, she told herself.

I don't want to be terrified of my own father.

I don't.

She pulled a light cotton robe over her pajamas, found her slippers in the cluttered closet, and stepped out into the hallway. It was hot and stuffy in the hall, almost suffocating. Pale morning light filtered down from the skylight overhead.

She stopped in front of Casey's room, wondering if she should wake him so that he could ask their father questions, too.

No, she decided. *The poor guy was up half the night. I'll let him sleep.*

Taking a deep breath, she walked the rest of the hall and stopped at her parents' bedroom. The door was open.

"Dad?"

No reply.

"Dad? Are you up?"

She stepped into the room. "Dad?"

He didn't seem to be there.

The air in here was heavy and smelled strangely sour. The curtains were drawn. The bedclothes were rumpled and tossed down at the foot of the bed. Margaret took a few more steps toward the bed.

"Dad?"

No. She had missed him. He was probably already locked in his basement workroom, she realized unhappily.

He must have gotten up very early and —

What was that in the bed?

Margaret clicked on a dresser lamp and stepped up beside the bed.

"Oh, no!" she cried, raising her hands to her face in horror.

The bedsheet was covered with a thick layer of dirt. Clumps of dirt.

Margaret stared down at it, not breathing, not moving.

The dirt was black and appeared to be moist.

And the dirt was moving.

Moving?

It can't be, Margaret thought. *That's impossible.*

She leaned down to take a closer look at the layer of dirt.

No. The dirt wasn't moving.

The dirt was filled with dozens of moving insects. And long brown earthworms. All crawling through the wet black clumps that lined her father's bed.

11

Casey didn't come downstairs until ten thirty. Before his arrival, Margaret had made herself breakfast, managed to pull on jeans and a T-shirt, had talked to Diane on the phone for half an hour, and had spent the rest of the time pacing back and forth in the living room, trying to decide what to do.

Desperate to talk to her dad, she had banged a few times on the basement door, timidly at first and then loudly. But he either couldn't hear her or chose not to. He didn't respond.

When Casey finally emerged, she poured him a tall glass of orange juice and led him out to the backyard to talk. It was a hazy day, the sky mostly yellow, the air already stifling hot even though the sun was still hovering low over the hills.

Walking toward the block of green shade cast by the hedges, she told her brother about their dad's green blood and about the insect-filled dirt in his bed.

Casey stood openmouthed, holding the glass of orange juice in front of him, untouched. He stared at Margaret and didn't say anything for a very long time.

Finally, he set the orange juice down on the lawn and said, "What should we do?" in a voice just above a whisper.

Margaret shrugged. "I wish Mom would call."

"Would you tell her everything?" Casey asked, shoving his hands deep into the pockets of his baggy shorts.

"I guess," Margaret said. "I don't know if she'd believe it, but —"

"It's so scary," Casey said. "I mean, he's our dad. We've known him our whole lives. I mean —"

"I know," Margaret said. "But he's not the same. He's —"

"Maybe he can explain it all," Casey said thoughtfully. "Maybe there's a good reason for everything. You know. Like the leaves on his head."

"We asked him about that," Margaret reminded her brother. "He just said it was a side effect. Not much of an explanation."

Casey nodded but didn't reply.

"I told some of it to Diane," Margaret admitted.

Casey looked up at her in surprise.

"Well, I had to tell *somebody*," she snapped edgily. "Diane thought I should call the police."

"Huh?" Casey shook his head. "Dad hasn't done anything wrong — has he? What would the police do?"

"I know," Margaret replied. "That's what I told Diane. But she said there's got to be some kind of law against being a mad scientist."

"Dad isn't a mad scientist," Casey said angrily. "That's stupid. He's just — He's just —"

Just what? Margaret thought. *What* is *he?*

A few hours later, they were still in the backyard, trying to figure out what to do, when the kitchen door opened and their father called them to come in.

Margaret looked at Casey in surprise. "I don't believe it. He came upstairs."

"Maybe we can talk to him," Casey said.

They both raced into the kitchen. Dr. Brewer, his Dodgers cap in place, flashed them a smile as he set two soup bowls down on the table. "Hi," he said brightly. "Lunchtime."

"Huh? You made lunch?" Casey exclaimed, unable to conceal his astonishment.

"Dad, we've got to talk," Margaret said seriously.

"Afraid I don't have much time," he said, avoiding her stare. "Sit down. Try this new dish. I want to see if you like it."

Margaret and Casey obediently took their places at the table. "What *is* this stuff?" Casey cried.

The two bowls were filled with a green, pulpy substance. "It looks like green mashed potatoes," Casey said, making a face.

"It's something different," Dr. Brewer said mysteriously, standing over them at the head of the table. "Go ahead. Taste it. I bet you'll be surprised."

"Dad — you've never made lunch for us before," Margaret said, trying to keep the suspicion out of her voice.

"I just wanted you to try this," he said, his smile fading. "You're my guinea pigs."

"We have some things we want to ask you," Margaret said, lifting her spoon but not eating the green mess.

"Your mother called this morning," their father said.

"When?" Margaret asked eagerly.

"Just a short while ago. I guess you were outside and didn't hear the phone ring."

"What did she say?" Casey asked, staring down at the bowl in front of him.

"Aunt Eleanor's doing better. She's been moved out of intensive care. Your mom may be able to come home soon."

"Great!" Margaret and Casey cried in unison.

"Eat," Dr. Brewer instructed, pointing to the bowls.

"Uh . . . aren't you going to have some?" Casey asked, rolling his spoon around in his fingers.

"No," their father replied quickly. "I already ate." He leaned with both hands against the tabletop. Margaret saw that his cut hand was freshly bandaged.

"Dad, last night —" she started.

But he cut her off. "Eat, will you? Try it."

"But what *is* it?" Casey demanded, whining. "It doesn't smell too good."

"I think you'll like the taste," Dr. Brewer insisted impatiently. "It should taste very sweet."

He stared at them, urging them to eat the green stuff.

Staring into the bowl at the mysterious substance, Margaret was suddenly frozen with fear. *He's too eager for us to eat this*, she thought, glancing up at her brother.

He's too desperate.

He's never made lunch before. Why did he make this?

And why won't he tell us what it is?

What's going on here? she wondered. And Casey's expression revealed that he was wondering the same thing.

Is Dad trying to do something to us? Is this green stuff going to change us, or hurt us . . . or make us grow leaves, too?

What crazy thoughts, Margaret realized.

But she also realized that she was terrified of whatever this stuff was he was trying to feed them.

"What's the matter with you two?" their father cried impatiently. He raised his hand in an eating gesture. "Pick up your spoons. Come on. What are you waiting for?"

Margaret and Casey raised their spoons and dropped them into the soft green substance. But they didn't raise the spoons to their mouths.

They couldn't.

"Eat! Eat!" Dr. Brewer screamed, pounding the table with his good hand. "What are you waiting for? Eat your lunch. Go ahead. Eat it!"

He's giving us no choice, Margaret thought.

Her hand was trembling as she reluctantly raised the spoon to her mouth.

"Go ahead. You'll like it," Dr. Brewer insisted, leaning over the table.

Casey watched as Margaret raised the spoon to her lips.

The doorbell rang.

"Who could that be?" Dr. Brewer asked, very annoyed at the interruption. "I'll be right back, kids." He lumbered out to the front hall.

"Saved by the bell," Margaret said, dropping the spoon back into the bowl with a sickening plop.

"This stuff is disgusting," Casey whispered. "It's some kind of plant food or something. Yuck!"

"Quick —" Margaret said, jumping up and grabbing the two bowls. "Help me."

They rushed to the sink, pulled out the wastebasket, and scooped the contents of both bowls into the garbage. Then they carried the bowls back to the table and set them down beside the spoons.

"Let's go see who's at the door," Casey said.

They crept into the hall in time to see a man carrying a black briefcase step into the front entranceway and greet their father with a short handshake. The man had a tanned bald head and was wearing large blue-lensed sunglasses. He had a brown mustache and was wearing a navy blue suit with a red and white striped tie.

"Mr. Martinez!" their father exclaimed. "What a . . . surprise."

"That's Dad's old boss from PolyTech," Margaret whispered to Casey.

"I *know*," Casey replied peevishly.

"I said weeks ago I'd come check up on how your work is coming along," Martinez said, sniffing the air for some reason. "Wellington gave me a lift. My car is in the garage — for a change."

"Well, I'm not really ready," Dr. Brewer stammered, looking very uncomfortable even from Margaret's vantage point behind him. "I wasn't expecting anyone. I mean . . . I don't think this is a good time."

"No problem. I'll just have a quick look," Martinez said, putting a hand on Dr. Brewer's shoulder as if to calm him. "I've always been so interested in your work. You know that. And you know that it wasn't *my* idea to let you go. The board forced me. They gave me no choice. But I'm not giving up on you. I promise you that.

Come on. Let's see what kind of progress you're making."

"Well . . ." Dr. Brewer couldn't hide his displeasure at Mr. Martinez's surprise appearance. He scowled and tried to block the path to the basement steps.

At least it seemed that way to Margaret, who watched silently beside her brother.

Mr. Martinez stepped past Dr. Brewer and pulled open the basement door. "Hi, guys." Mr. Martinez gave the two kids a wave, hoisting his briefcase as if it weighed two tons.

Their father looked surprised to see them there. "Did you kids finish your lunch?"

"Yeah, it was pretty good," Casey lied.

The answer seemed to please Dr. Brewer. Adjusting the brim of his Dodgers cap, he followed Mr. Martinez into the basement, carefully closing and locking the door behind him.

"Maybe he'll give Dad his job back," Casey said, walking back into the kitchen. He pulled open the refrigerator to look for something for lunch.

"Don't be stupid," Margaret said, reaching over him to pull out a container of egg salad. "If Dad really is growing plants that are part animal, he'll be famous. He won't need a job."

"Yeah, I guess," Casey said thoughtfully. "Is that all there is? Just egg salad?"

"I'll make you a sandwich," Margaret offered.

"I'm not really hungry," Casey replied. "That green stuff made me sick. Why do you think he wanted us to eat it?"

"I don't know," Margaret said. She put a hand on Casey's slender shoulder. "I'm really scared, Casey. I wish Mom were home."

"Me, too," he said quietly.

Margaret put the egg salad back into the refrigerator. She closed the door, then leaned her hot forehead against it. "Casey —"

"What?"

"Do you think Dad is telling us the truth?"

"About what?"

"About *anything*?"

"I don't know," Casey said, shaking his head. Then his expression suddenly changed. "There's one way to find out," he said, his eyes lighting up.

"Huh? What do you mean?" Margaret pushed herself away from the refrigerator.

"The first chance we get, the first time Dad is away," Casey whispered, "let's go back down in the basement and see for ourselves what he's doing."

13

They got their chance the next afternoon when their father emerged from the basement, red metal tool chest in hand. "I promised Mr. Henry next door I'd help him install a new sink in his bathroom," he explained, adjusting his Dodgers cap with his free hand.

"When are you coming back?" Casey asked, glancing at Margaret.

Not very subtle, Casey, Margaret thought, rolling her eyes.

"It shouldn't take more than a couple of hours," Dr. Brewer said. He disappeared out the kitchen door.

They watched him cut through the hedges in the backyard and head to Mr. Henry's back door. "It's now or never," Margaret said, glancing doubtfully at Casey. "Think we can do this?" She tried the door. Locked, as usual.

"No problem," Casey said, a mischievous grin spreading across his face. "Go get a paper clip.

I'll show you what my friend Kevin taught me last week."

Margaret obediently found a paper clip on her desk and brought it to him. Casey straightened the clip out, then poked it into the lock. In a few seconds, he hummed a triumphant fanfare and pulled the door open.

"Now you're an expert lock picker, huh? Your friend Kevin is a good guy to know," Margaret said, shaking her head.

Casey grinned and motioned for Margaret to go first.

"Okay. Let's not think about it. Let's just do it," Margaret said, summoning her courage and stepping onto the landing.

A few seconds later, they were in the basement.

Knowing a little of what to expect down here didn't make it any less frightening. They were hit immediately by a blast of steamy, hot air. The air, Margaret realized, was so wet, so thick, that droplets immediately clung to her skin.

Squinting against the sudden bright light, they stopped in the doorway to the plant room. The plants seemed taller, thicker, more plentiful than the first time they had ventured down here.

Long, sinewy tendrils drooped from thick yellow stalks. Broad green and yellow leaves bobbed and trembled, shimmering under the white light. Leaves slapped against each other, making a soft, wet sound. A fat tomato plopped to the ground.

Everything seemed to shimmer. The plants all seemed to quiver expectantly. They weren't standing still. They seemed to be reaching up, reaching out, quaking with energy as they grew.

Long brown tendrils snaked along the dirt, wrapping themselves around other plants, around each other. A bushy fern had grown to the ceiling, curved, and started its way back down again.

"Wow!" Casey cried, impressed with this trembling, glistening jungle. "Are all these plants really brand-new?"

"I guess so," Margaret said softly. "They look prehistoric!"

They heard breathing sounds, loud sighing, a low moan coming from the direction of the supply closet against the wall.

A tendril suddenly swung out from a long stalk. Margaret pulled Casey back. "Look out. Don't get too close," she warned.

"I know," he said sharply, moving away from her. "Don't grab me like that. You scared me."

The tendril slid harmlessly to the dirt.

"Sorry," she said, squeezing his shoulder affectionately. "It's just . . . well, you remember last time."

"I'll be careful," he said.

Margaret shuddered.

She heard breathing. Steady, quiet breathing.

These plants are definitely not normal, she

84

thought. She took a step back, letting her eyes roam over the amazing jungle of slithering, sighing plants.

She was still staring at them when she heard Casey's terrified scream.

"Help! It's got me! It's *got* me!"

Margaret uttered a shriek of terror and spun away from the plants to find her brother.

"Help!" Casey cried.

Gripped with fear, Margaret took a few steps toward Casey, then saw the small gray creature scampering across the floor.

She started to laugh.

"Casey, it's a squirrel!"

"What?" His voice was several octaves higher than normal. "It — it grabbed my ankle and —"

"Look," Margaret said, pointing. "It's a squirrel. Look how scared it is. It must have run right into you."

"Oh." Casey sighed. The color began to return to his ash-gray face. "I thought it was a . . . plant."

"Right. A furry gray plant," Margaret said, shaking her head. Her heart was still thudding in her chest. "You sure gave me a scare, Casey."

The squirrel stopped several yards away, turned, stood up on its hind legs, and stared back at them, quivering all over.

"How did a squirrel get down here?" Casey demanded, his voice still shaky.

Margaret shrugged. "Squirrels are always getting in," she said. "And remember that chipmunk we couldn't get rid of?" Then she glanced over to the small ground-level window at the top of the opposite wall. "That window — it's open," she told Casey. "The squirrel must have climbed in over there."

"*Shoo!*" Casey yelled at the squirrel. He started to chase it. The squirrel's tail shot right up in the air and then it took off, running through the tangled plants. "Get out! Get out!" Casey screamed.

The terrified squirrel, with Casey in close pursuit, circled the plants twice. Then it headed to the far wall, leaped onto a carton, then onto a higher carton, then bounded out the open window.

Casey stopped running and stared up at the window.

"Good work," Margaret said. "Now, let's get out of here. We don't know what anything is. We have no idea what to look for. So we can't tell if Dad is telling the truth or not."

She started toward the stairs but stopped when she heard the bumping sound. "Casey —

did you hear that?" She searched for her brother, but he was hidden by the thick leaves of the plants. "Casey?"

"Yeah. I heard it," he answered, still out of her view. "It's coming from the supply closet."

The loud thumping made Margaret shudder. It sounded to her exactly like someone banging on the closet wall.

"Casey, let's check it out," she said.

No reply.

The banging got louder.

"Casey?"

Why wasn't he answering her?

"Casey — where *are* you? You're frightening me," Margaret called, moving closer to the shimmering plants. Another tomato plopped to the ground, so near her foot, it made her jump.

Despite the intense heat, she suddenly felt cold all over.

"Casey?"

"Margaret — come here. I've found something," he finally said. He sounded uncertain, worried.

She hurried around the plants and saw him standing in front of the worktable beside the supply closet. The banging from the closet had stopped.

"Casey, what's the matter? You scared me," Margaret scolded. She stopped and leaned against the wooden worktable.

"Look," her brother said, holding up a dark, folded-up bundle. "I found this. On the floor. Shoved under this worktable."

"Huh? What is it?" Margaret asked.

Casey unfolded it. It was a suit jacket. A blue suit jacket. A red and white striped necktie was folded inside it.

"It's Mr. Martinez's," Casey said, squeezing the collar of the wrinkled jacket between his hands. "It's his jacket and tie."

Margaret's mouth dropped open into a wide O of surprise. "You mean he left it here?"

"If he left it, why was it bundled up and shoved back under the table?" Casey asked.

Margaret stared at the jacket. She ran her hand over the silky striped tie.

"Did you see Mr. Martinez leave the house yesterday afternoon?" Casey asked.

"No," Margaret answered. "But he *must* have left. I mean, his car was gone."

"He didn't drive, remember? He told Dad he got a lift."

Margaret raised her eyes from the wrinkled jacket to her brother's worried face. "Casey — what are you saying? That Mr. Martinez didn't leave? That he was eaten by a plant or something? That's ridiculous!"

"Then why were his coat and tie hidden like that?" Casey demanded.

Margaret didn't have a chance to respond.

They both gasped as they heard loud footsteps on the stairs.

Someone was hurrying down to the basement.

"Hide!" Margaret whispered.

"Where?" Casey asked, his eyes wide with panic.

15

Margaret leaped up onto the carton, then pulled herself through the small open window. A tight squeeze, but she struggled out onto the grass. Then she turned around to help Casey.

That squirrel turned out to be a friend, she thought, tugging her brother's arms as he scrambled out of the basement. *It showed us the only escape route.*

The afternoon air felt quite cool compared to the steamy basement. Breathing hard, they both squatted down to peer into the window. "Who is it?" Casey whispered.

Margaret didn't have to answer. They both saw their father step into the white light, his eyes searching the plant room.

"Why did Dad come back?" Casey asked.

"Sshhh!" Margaret held her finger to her lips. Then she climbed to her feet and pulled Casey toward the back door. "Come on. Hurry."

The back door was unlocked. They stepped into

the kitchen just as their father emerged from the basement, a concerned expression on his face. "Hey — *there* you are!" he exclaimed.

"Hi, Dad," Margaret said, trying to sound casual. "Why'd you come back?"

"Had to get more tools," he answered, studying their faces. He eyed them suspiciously. "Where *were* you two?"

"Out in the backyard," Margaret said quickly. "We came in when we heard the back door slam."

Dr. Brewer scowled and shook his head. "You never used to lie to me before," he said. "I know you went down into the basement again. You left the door wide open."

"We just wanted to look," Casey said quickly, glancing at Margaret, his expression fearful.

"We found Mr. Martinez's jacket and tie," Margaret said. "What happened to him, Dad?"

"Huh?" The question seemed to catch Dr. Brewer by surprise.

"Why did he leave his jacket and tie down there?" Margaret asked.

"I'm raising two snoops," her father griped. "Martinez got hot, okay? I have to keep the basement at a very high, tropical temperature with lots of humidity. Martinez became uncomfortable. He removed his jacket and tie and put them down on the worktable. Then he forgot them when he left."

Dr. Brewer chuckled. "I think he was in a state of shock from everything I showed him down there. It's no wonder he forgot his things. But I called Martinez this morning. I'm going to drive over and return his stuff when I finish at Mr. Henry's."

Margaret saw a smile break out on Casey's face. She felt relieved, too. It was good to know that Mr. Martinez was okay.

How awful to suspect my own father of doing something terrible to someone, she thought.

But she couldn't help herself. The fear returned every time she saw him.

"I'd better get going," Dr. Brewer said. Carrying the tools he had picked up, he started toward the back door. But he stopped at the end of the hall and turned around. "Don't go back in the basement, okay? It really could be dangerous. You could be very sorry."

Margaret listened to the screen door slam behind him.

Was that a warning — or a threat? she wondered.

16

Margaret spent Saturday morning biking up in the golden hills with Diane. The sun burned through the morning smog, and the skies turned blue. A strong breeze kept them from getting too hot. The narrow road was lined with red and yellow wildflowers, and Margaret felt as if she were traveling somewhere far, far away.

They had lunch at Diane's house — tomato soup and avocado salad — then wandered back to Margaret's house, trying to figure out how to spend the rest of a beautiful afternoon.

Dr. Brewer was just backing the station wagon down the drive as Margaret and Diane rode up on their bikes. He rolled down the window, a broad smile on his face. "Good news!" he shouted. "Your mom is on her way home. I'm going to the airport to get her!"

"Oh, that's great!" Margaret exclaimed, so happy she could almost cry. Margaret and Diane waved and pedaled up the driveway.

I'm so happy, Margaret thought. *It'll be so good to have her back. Someone I can talk to. Someone who can explain . . . about Dad.*

They looked through some old copies of *Seventeen* and *People* in Margaret's room, listening to some music that Margaret had recently bought. At a little past three, Diane suddenly remembered that she had a makeup piano lesson that she was late for. She rushed out of the house in a panic, jumped on her bike, yelled, "Say hi to your mom for me!" and disappeared down the drive.

Margaret stood behind the house, looking out at the rolling hills, wondering what to do next to make the time pass before her mother got home. The strong, swirling breeze felt cool against her face. She decided to get a book and go sit down with it under the shady sassafras tree in the middle of the yard.

She turned and pulled open the kitchen door, and Casey came running up. "Where are our kites?" he asked, out of breath.

"Kites? I don't know. Why?" Margaret asked. "Hey —" She grabbed his shoulder to get his attention. "Mom's coming home. She should be here in an hour or so."

"Great!" he cried. "Just enough time to fly some kites. It's so windy. Come on. Want to fly 'em with me?"

"Sure," Margaret said. It would help pass the time. She thought hard, trying to remember where they put the kites. "Are they in the garage?"

"No," Casey told her. "I know. They're in the basement. On those shelves. The string, too." He pushed past her into the house. "I'll jimmy the lock and go down and get them."

"Hey, Casey — be careful down there," she called after him. He disappeared into the hallway. Margaret had second thoughts. She didn't want Casey down there in the plant room by himself. "Wait up," she called. "I'll come with you."

They made their way down the stairs quickly, into the hot, steamy air, into the bright lights.

The plants seemed to bend toward them, to reach out to them as they walked by. Margaret tried to ignore them. Walking right behind Casey, she kept her eyes on the tall metal shelves straight ahead.

The shelves were deep and filled with old, unwanted toys, games, and sports equipment, a plastic tent, some old sleeping bags. Casey got there first and started rummaging around on the lower shelves. "I know they're here somewhere," he said.

"Yeah. I remember storing them here," Margaret said, running her eyes over the top shelves.

Casey, down on his knees, started pulling boxes off the bottom shelf. Suddenly, he stopped. "Whoa — Margaret."

"Huh?" She took a step back. "What is it?"

"Look at this," Casey said softly. He pulled something out from behind the shelves, then stood up with it bundled in his hands.

Margaret saw that he was holding a pair of black shoes. And a pair of blue trousers.

Blue suit trousers?

His face suddenly pale, his features drawn, Casey let the shoes drop to the floor. He unfurled the trousers and held them up in front of him.

"Hey — look in the back pocket," Margaret said, pointing.

Casey reached into the back pocket and pulled out a black leather wallet.

"I don't believe this," Margaret said.

Casey's hands trembled as he opened the wallet and searched inside. He pulled out a green American Express card and read the name on it.

"It belongs to Mr. Martinez," he said, swallowing hard. He raised his eyes to Margaret's. This is Mr. Martinez's stuff."

17

"Dad lied," Casey said, staring in horror at the wallet in his hands. "Mr. Martinez might leave without his jacket. But he wouldn't leave without his pants and shoes."

"But — what *happened* to him?" Margaret asked, feeling sick.

Casey slammed the wallet shut. He shook his head sadly but didn't reply.

In the center of the room, a plant seemed to groan, the sound startling the two kids.

"Dad lied," Casey repeated, staring down at the pants and shoes on the floor. "Dad lied to us."

"What are we going to *do*?" Margaret cried, panic and desperation in her voice. "We've got to tell someone what's happening here. But who?"

The plant groaned again. Tendrils snaked along the dirt. Leaves clapped against each other softly, wetly.

And then the banging began again in the supply closet next to the shelves.

Margaret stared at Casey. "That thumping. What is it?"

They both listened to the insistent banging sounds. A low moan issued from the closet, followed by a higher-pitched one, both mournful, both very human-sounding.

"I think someone's *in* there!" Margaret exclaimed.

"Maybe it's Mr. Martinez," Casey suggested, still gripping the wallet tightly in his hand.

Thud thud thud.

"Do you think we should open the closet?" Casey asked timidly.

A plant groaned as if answering.

"Yes. I think we should," Margaret replied, suddenly cold all over. "If it's Mr. Martinez in there, we've got to let him out."

Casey set the wallet down on the shelf. Then they moved quickly to the supply closet.

Across from them, the plants seemed to shift and move as the two kids did. They heard breathing sounds, another groan, scurrying noises. Leaves bristled on their stalks. Tendrils drooped and slid.

"Hey — look!" Casey cried.

"I see," Margaret said. The closet door wasn't just locked. A two-by-four had been nailed over it.

Thud thud. Thud thud thud.

"There's someone in there — I *know* it!" Margaret cried.

"I'll get the hammer," Casey said. Keeping close to the wall and as far away from the plants as he could, he edged his way toward the worktable.

A few seconds later, he returned with a claw hammer.

Thud thud.

Working together, they pried the two-by-four off the door. It clattered noisily to the floor.

The banging from inside the supply closet grew louder, more insistent.

"Now what do we do about the lock?" Margaret asked, staring at it.

Casey scratched his head. They both had perspiration dripping down their faces. The steamy, hot air made it hard to catch their breaths.

"I don't know how to unlock it," Casey said, stumped.

"What if we tried to pry the door off the way we pulled off the two-by-four?" Margaret asked.

Thud thud thud.

Casey shrugged. "I don't know. Let's try."

Working the claw of the hammer into the narrow crack, they tried prying the door on the side of the lock. When it wouldn't budge, they moved to the hinged side of the door and tried there.

"It's not moving," Casey said, mopping his forehead with his arm.

"Keep trying," Margaret said. "Here. Let's both push it."

Digging the claw in just above the lower hinge, they both pushed the handle of the hammer with all their strength.

"It — it moved a little," Margaret said, breathing hard.

They kept at it. The wet wood began to crack. They both pushed against the hammer, wedging the claw into the crack.

Finally, with a loud ripping sound, they managed to pull the door off.

"Huh?" Casey dropped the hammer.

They both squinted into the dark closet.

And screamed in horror when they saw what was inside.

101

"Look!" Margaret cried, her heart thudding. She suddenly felt dizzy. She gripped the side of the closet to steady herself.

"I — don't believe this," Casey said quietly, his voice trembling as he stared into the long, narrow supply closet.

They both gaped at the weird plants that filled the closet.

Were they plants?

Under the dim ceiling bulb, they bent and writhed, groaning, breathing, sighing. Branches shook, leaves shimmered and moved, tall plants leaned forward as if reaching out to Margaret and Casey.

"Look at that one!" Casey cried, taking a step back, stumbling into Margaret. "It has an arm!"

"Ohh." Margaret followed Casey's stare. Casey was right. The tall, leafy plant appeared to have a green human arm descending from its stalk.

Margaret's eyes darted around the closet. To her horror, she realized that several plants seemed to have human features — green arms, a yellow hand with three fingers poking from it, two stumpy legs where the stem should be.

She and her brother both cried out when they saw the plant with the face. Inside a cluster of broad leaves there appeared to grow a round, green tomato. But the tomato had a human-shaped nose and an open mouth, from which it repeatedly uttered the most mournful sighs and groans.

Another plant, a short plant with clusters of broad, oval leaves, had two green, nearly human faces partly hidden by the leaves, both wailing through open mouths.

"Let's get out of here!" Casey cried, grabbing Margaret's hand in fear and tugging her away from the closet. "This is — gross!"

The plants moaned and sighed. Green, finger-less hands reached out to Margaret and Casey. A yellow, sick-looking plant near the wall made choking sounds. A tall flowering plant stag-gered toward them, thin, tendril-like arms outstretched.

"Wait!" Margaret cried, pulling her hand out of Casey's. She spotted something on the closet floor behind the moaning, shifting plants. "Casey — what's that?" she asked, pointing.

She struggled to focus her eyes in the dim light of the closet. On the floor behind the plants, near the shelves on the back wall, were two human feet.

Margaret stepped cautiously into the closet. The feet, she saw, were attached to legs.

"Margaret — let's go!" Casey pleaded.

"No. Look. There's someone back there," Margaret said, staring hard.

"Huh?"

"A person. Not a plant," Margaret said. She took another step. A soft green arm brushed against her side.

"Margaret, what are you doing?" Casey asked, his voice high and frightened.

"I have to see who it is," Margaret said.

She took a deep breath and held it. Then, ignoring the moans, the sighs, the green arms reaching out to her, the hideous green-tomato faces, she plunged through the plants to the back of the closet.

"Dad!" she cried.

Her father was lying on the floor, his hands and feet tied tightly with plant tendrils, his mouth gagged by a wide strip of elastic tape.

"Margaret —" Casey was beside her. He lowered his eyes to the floor. "Oh, no!"

104

Their father stared up at them, pleading with his eyes. *"Mmmmm!"* he cried, struggling to talk through the gag.

Margaret dived to the floor and started to untie him.

"No — stop!" Casey cried, and pulled her back by the shoulders.

"Casey, let go of me. What's wrong with you?" Margaret cried angrily. "It's Dad. He —"

"It can't be Dad!" Casey said, still holding her by the shoulders. "Dad is at the airport — remember?"

Behind them, the plants seemed to be moaning in unison, a terrifying chorus. A tall plant fell over and rolled toward the open closet door.

"Mmmmmmm!" their father continued to plead, struggling at the tendrils that imprisoned him.

"I've got to untie him," Margaret told her brother. "Let go of me."

"No," Casey insisted. "Margaret — look at his head."

Margaret turned her eyes to her father's head. He was bareheaded. No Dodgers cap. He had tufts of green leaves growing where his hair should be.

"We've already seen that," Margaret snapped. "It's a side effect, remember?" She reached down to pull at her father's restraints.

"No — don't!" Casey insisted.

"Okay, okay," Margaret said. "I'll just pull the tape off his mouth. I won't untie him."

She reached down and tugged at the elastic tape until she managed to get it off.

"Kids — I'm so glad to see you," Dr. Brewer said. "Quick! Untie me."

"How did you get in here?" Casey demanded, standing above him, hands on his hips, staring down at him suspiciously. "We saw you leave for the airport."

"That wasn't me," Dr. Brewer said. "I've been locked in here for days."

"Huh?" Casey cried.

"But we saw you —" Margaret started.

"It wasn't me. It's a plant," Dr. Brewer said. "It's a plant copy of me."

"Dad —" Casey said.

"Please. There's no time to explain," their father said urgently, raising his leaf-covered head to look quickly toward the closet doorway. "Just untie me. Quick!"

"The father we've been living with? He's a plant?" Margaret cried, swallowing hard.

"Yes. Please — untie me!"

Margaret reached for the tendrils.

"No!" Casey insisted. "How do we know you're telling the truth?"

"I'll explain everything. I promise," he pleaded.

"Hurry. Our lives are at stake. Mr. Martinez is in here, too."

Startled, Margaret turned her eyes to the far wall. Sure enough, Mr. Martinez also lay on the floor, bound and gagged.

"Let me out — please!" her father cried.

Margaret couldn't stand it anymore. "I'm untying him," she told Casey, and bent down to start grappling with the tendrils.

Her father sighed gratefully. Casey bent down and reluctantly began working at the tendrils, too.

Finally, they had loosened them enough so their father could slip out. He climbed to his feet slowly, stretching his arms, moving his legs, bending his knees. "Man, that feels good," he said, giving Margaret and Casey a grim smile.

"Dad — should we untie Mr. Martinez?" Margaret asked.

But without warning, Dr. Brewer pushed past the two kids and made his way out of the closet.

"Dad — whoa! Where are you going?" Margaret called.

"You said you'd explain everything!" Casey insisted. He and his sister ran through the moaning plants, following their father.

"I will. I will." Breathing hard, Dr. Brewer strode quickly to the woodpile against the far wall. Margaret and Casey both gasped as he picked up an axe.

He spun around to face them, holding the thick axe handle with both hands. His face frozen with determination, he started toward them.

"Dad — what are you *doing*?" Margaret cried.

19

Swinging the axe onto his shoulder, Dr. Brewer advanced on Margaret and Casey. He groaned from the effort of raising the heavy tool, his face reddening, his eyes wide, excited.

"Dad, please!" Margaret cried, gripping Casey's shoulder, backing up toward the jungle of plants in the center of the room.

"What are you *doing*?" she repeated.

"He's not our real father!" Casey cried. "I *told* you we shouldn't untie him!"

"He *is* our real father!" Margaret insisted. I *know* he is!" She turned her eyes to her father, looking for an answer.

But he stared back at them, his face filled with confusion — and menace, the axe in his hands gleaming under the bright ceiling lights.

"Dad — answer us!" Margaret demanded. "Answer us!"

Before Dr. Brewer could reply, they heard loud, rapid footsteps clumping down the basement steps.

All three of them turned to the doorway of the plant room — to see an alarmed-looking Dr. Brewer enter. He grabbed the bill of his Dodgers cap as he strode angrily toward the two kids.

"What are you two doing down here?" he cried. "You promised me. Here's your mother. Don't you want to — ?"

Mrs. Brewer appeared at his side. She started to call out a greeting but stopped, freezing in horror when she saw the confusing scene.

"No!" she screamed, seeing the other Dr. Brewer, the capless Dr. Brewer, holding an axe in front of him with both hands. "No!" Her face filled with horror. She turned to the Dr. Brewer that had just brought her home.

He glared accusingly at Margaret and Casey. "What have you *done*? You let him escape?"

"He's our dad," Margaret said, in a tiny little voice she barely recognized.

"*I'm* your dad!" the Dr. Brewer at the doorway bellowed. "Not him! He's not your dad. He's not even human! He's a plant!"

Margaret and Casey both gasped and drew back in terror.

"*You're* the plant!" the bareheaded Dr. Brewer accused, raising the axe.

110

"He's dangerous!" the other Dr. Brewer exclaimed. "How could you have let him out?"

Caught in the middle, Margaret and Casey stared from one father to the other.

Who was their *real* father?

20

"That's not your father!" Dr. Brewer with the Dodgers cap cried again, moving into the room. "He's a copy. A plant copy. One of my experiments that went wrong. I locked him in the supply closet because he's dangerous."

"*You're* the copy!" the other Dr. Brewer accused, and raised the axe again.

Margaret and Casey stood motionless, exchanging terrified glances.

"Kids — what have you done?" Mrs. Brewer cried, her hands pressed against her cheeks, her eyes wide with disbelief.

"What *have* we done?" Margaret asked her brother in a low voice.

Staring wide-eyed from one man to the other, Casey seemed too frightened to reply.

"I — I don't know what to do," Casey managed to whisper.

What can *we do?* Margaret wondered silently, realizing that her entire body was trembling.

"He has to be destroyed!" the axe-wielding Dr. Brewer shouted, staring at his look-alike across the room.

Beside them, plants quivered and shook, sighing loudly. Tendrils slithered across the dirt. Leaves shimmered and whispered.

"Put down the axe. You're not fooling anyone," the other Dr. Brewer said.

"You have to be destroyed!" Dr. Brewer with no cap repeated, his eyes wild, his face scarlet, moving closer, the axe gleaming as if electrified under the white light.

Dad would never act like this, Margaret realized. *Casey and I were idiots. We let him out of the closet. And now he's going to kill our real dad. And mom.*

And then . . . us!

What can I do? she wondered, trying to think clearly even though her mind was whirring wildly out of control.

What can I do?

Uttering a desperate cry of protest, Margaret leaped forward and grabbed the axe from the imposter's hands.

He gaped in surprise as she steadied her grip on the handle. It was heavier than she'd imagined. "Get back!" she screamed. "Get back — now!"

"Margaret — wait!" her mother cried, still too frightened to move from the doorway.

The capless Dr. Brewer reached for the axe.

"Give it back to me! You don't know what you're doing!" he pleaded, and made a wild grab for it.

Margaret pulled back and swung the axe. "Stay back. *Everyone*, stay back."

"Thank goodness!" Dr. Brewer with the Dodgers cap exclaimed. "We've got to get him back in the closet. He's very dangerous." He stepped up to Margaret. "Give *me* the axe."

Margaret hesitated.

"Give *me* the axe," he insisted.

Margaret turned to her mother. "What should I do?"

Mrs. Brewer shrugged helplessly. "I — I don't know."

"Princess — don't do it," the capless Dr. Brewer said softly, staring into Margaret's eyes.

He called me Princess, Margaret realized.

The other one never had.

Does this mean that the dad in the closet is my real dad?

"Margaret — give me the axe." The one in the cap made a grab for it.

Margaret backed away and swung the axe again.

"Get back! Both of you — stay back!" she warned.

"I'm warning you," Dr. Brewer in the cap said. "He's dangerous. Listen to me, Margaret."

"Get back!" she repeated, desperately trying to decide what to do.

Which one is my real dad?
Which one? Which one? Which one?

Her eyes darting back and forth from one to the other, she saw that each of them had a bandage around his right hand. And it gave her an idea.

"Casey, there's a knife on the wall over there," she said, still holding the axe poised. "Get it for me — fast!"

Casey obediently hurried to the wall. It took him a short while to find the knife among all the tools hanging there. He reached up on tiptoe to pull it down, then hurried back to Margaret with it.

Margaret lowered the axe and took the long-bladed knife from him.

"Margaret — give me the axe," the man in the Dodgers cap insisted impatiently.

"Margaret, what are you doing?" the man from the supply closet asked, suddenly looking frightened.

"I — I have an idea," Margaret said hesitantly.

She took a deep breath.

Then she stepped over to the man from the supply closet and pushed the knife blade into his arm.

"Ow!" he cried out as the blade cut through the skin.

Margaret pulled the knife back, having made a tiny puncture hole.

Red blood trickled from the hole.

"He's our real dad," she told Casey, sighing with relief. "Here, Dad." She handed him the axe.

"Margaret — you're wrong!" the man in the baseball cap cried in alarm. "He's tricked you! He's *tricked* you!"

The capless Dr. Brewer moved quickly. He picked up the axe, took three steps forward, pulled the axe back, and swung with all his might.

The Dr. Brewer in the cap opened his mouth wide and uttered a hushed cry of alarm. The cry was choked off as the axe cut easily through his body, slicing him in two.

A thick green liquid oozed from the wound. And as the man fell, his mouth locking open in disbelief and horror, Margaret could see that his body was actually a stem. He had no bones, no human organs.

The body thudded to the floor. Green liquid puddled around it.

"Princess — we're okay!" Dr. Brewer cried, flinging the axe aside. "You guessed right!"

"It wasn't a guess," Margaret said, sinking into his arms. "I remembered the green blood. I saw it. Late at night. One of you was in the bathroom, bleeding green blood. I knew my real dad would have red blood."

"We're okay!" Mrs. Brewer cried, rushing into her husband's arms. "We're okay. We're all okay!"

All four of them rushed together in an emotional family hug.

"One more thing we have to do," their father said, his arms around the two kids. "Let's get Mr. Martinez out of the closet."

By dinnertime, things had almost returned to normal.

They had finally managed to welcome their mother home and tried to explain to her all that had happened in her absence.

Mr. Martinez had been rescued from the supply

closet, not too much the worse for wear. He and Dr. Brewer had had a long discussion about what had happened and about Dr. Brewer's work.

He expressed total bewilderment as to what Dr. Brewer had accomplished, but he knew enough to realize that it was historic. "Perhaps you need the structured environment the lab on campus offers. I'll talk to the board members about getting you back on staff," Mr. Martinez said. It was his way of inviting their father back to work.

After Mr. Martinez was driven home, Dr. Brewer disappeared into the basement for about an hour. He returned grim-faced and exhausted. "I destroyed most of the plants," he explained, sinking into an armchair. "I had to. They were suffering. Later, I'll destroy the rest."

"Every single plant?" Mrs. Brewer asked.

"Well . . . there are a few normal ones that I can plant out back in the garden," he replied. He shook his head sadly. "Only a few."

At dinner, he finally had the strength to explain to Margaret, Casey, and Mrs. Brewer what had happened down in the basement.

"I was working on a super plant," he said, "trying to electronically make a new plant using DNA elements from other plants. Then I accidentally cut my hand on a slide. I didn't realize it, but some of my blood got mixed in with the plant molecules I was using. When I turned on the machine, my molecules got mixed in with plant molecules — and I ended up with something that was part human, part plant."

"That's gross!" Casey exclaimed, dropping a forkful of mashed potatoes.

"Well, I'm a scientist," Dr. Brewer replied, "so I didn't think it was gross. I thought it was pretty exciting. I mean, here I was, inventing an entirely new kind of creature."

"Those plants with faces —" Margaret started.

Her father nodded. "Yes. Those were things I made by inserting human materials into plant materials. I kept putting them in the supply closet. I got carried away. I didn't know how far I could go, how human I could make the plants. I could see that my creations were unhappy, suffering. But I couldn't stop. It was too exciting."

He took a long drink of water from his glass.

"You didn't tell me any of this," Mrs. Brewer said, shaking her head.

"I couldn't," he said. "I couldn't tell anyone. I — I was too involved. Then one day, I went too far. I created a plant that was an exact copy of me in almost every way. He looked like me. He sounded like me. And he had my brain, my mind."

"But he still acted like a plant in some ways," Margaret said. "He ate plant food and —"

"He wasn't perfect," Dr. Brewer said, leaning forward over the dinner table, talking in a low, serious voice. "He had flaws. But he was strong enough and smart enough to overpower me, to lock me in the closet, to take my place — and to continue my experiments. And when Mr. Martinez arrived unexpectedly, he locked him in the closet, too, so that his secret would be safe."

"Was the head full of leaves one of the flaws?" Casey asked.

Dr. Brewer nodded. "Yes, he was almost a perfect clone of me, almost a perfect human, but not quite."

"But, Dad," Margaret said, pointing, "you have leaves on your head, too."

He reached up and pulled one off. "I know," he said, making a disgusted face. "That's really gross, huh?"

Everyone agreed.

"Well, when I cut my hand, some of the plant materials mixed with my blood, got into my system," he explained. "And then I turned on the machine. The machine created a strong chemical reaction between the plant materials and my blood. Then, my hair fell out overnight. And the leaves immediately started to sprout. Don't worry, guys. The leaves are falling out already. I think my hair will grow back."

Margaret and Casey cheered.

"I guess things will return to normal around here," Mrs. Brewer said, smiling at her husband.

"Better than normal," he said, smiling back. "If Mr. Martinez convinces the board to give me my job back, I'll clear out the basement and turn it into the best game room you ever saw!"

Margaret and Casey cheered again.

"We're all alive and safe," Dr. Brewer said, hugging both kids at once. "Thanks to you two."

It was the happiest dinner Margaret could remember. After they cleaned up, they all went out for ice cream. It was nearly ten o'clock when they returned.

Dr. Brewer headed for the basement.

"Hey — where are you going?" his wife called suspiciously.

"I'm just going down to deal with the rest of the plants," Dr. Brewer assured her. "I want to make sure that everything is gone, that this horrible chapter in our lives is over."

By the end of the week, most of the plants had been destroyed. A giant pile of leaves, roots, and stalks were burned in a bonfire that lasted for hours. A few tiny plants had been transplanted outside. All of the equipment had been dismantled and trucked to the university.

On Saturday, all four Brewers went to select a pool table for the new basement rec room. On

Sunday, Margaret found herself standing in back by the garden, staring up at the golden hills.

It's so peaceful now, she thought happily.

So peaceful here. And so beautiful.

The smile faded from her face when she heard the whisper at her feet. "Margaret."

She looked down to see a small yellow flower nudging her ankle.

"Margaret," the flower whispered, "help me. Please — help me. I'm your father. Really! I'm your real father."

BEHIND THE SCREAMS

STAY OUT OF THE BASEMENT

CONTENTS

About the Author

Q & A with R.L. Stine

Double Trouble: Cloned Animals

Monsters of Matter and Mind

Creepy Candle

The Good, the Bad, and the Ugly

A Terrifying Peek at
GOOSEBUMPS HALL OF HORRORS #5:
DON'T SCREAM!

Bonus material written and compiled
by Gabrielle S. Balkan

About the Author

R.L. Stine's books are read all over the world. So far, his books have sold more than 300 million copies, making him one of the most popular children's authors in history. Besides Goosebumps, R.L. Stine has written the teen series Fear Street, the funny series Rotten School, as well as the Mostly Ghostly series, The Nightmare Room series, and the two-book thriller *Dangerous Girls*. R.L. Stine lives in New York with his wife, Jane, and Minnie, his King Charles spaniel. You can learn more about him at www.RLStine.com.

Q & A with R.L. Stine

Why is it so scary to walk down into a dark basement?

R.L. Stine (RLS): *Anything could be lurking down there. There are cobwebs and scampering mice. And the dripping, creaking sounds help add to the scary atmosphere. And who's behind the furnace making that sound of heavy breathing? YIKES! I'm scaring MYSELF!*

What kind of creepy things are hiding in your basement?

RLS: *My basement is just like everybody's basement. It's filled with the stuff everyone keeps around—old books, old clothes, a few coffins, a decaying mummy, jars of zombie dust, bat blood . . . all the usual stuff.*

Have you ever had a dream or a nightmare about a character from one of your books?

RLS: *I never have nightmares. Never. My dreams are very boring. I guess it's because I'm too busy dreaming up nightmares for kids during the day.*

Have you ever come up with the ending to a story before having any other part of it figured out?

RLS: *Writers most from different am I. first ending the—backwards write I.*

In Goosebumps: Hall of Horrors #5: *Don't Scream!* there is a cell phone with a mind of its own. Will the robots eventually take over the world?

RLS: *Machines have already taken over. A robot beat all the human contestants on* Jeopardy! *Humans can't go anywhere without having a cell phone attached to their ear. The machines are winning—which is GREAT news for a horror writer like me!*

Double Trouble: Cloned Animals

What do Dolly the sheep, Copycat the . . . cat, Gene the calf, and Snuppy the Afghan hound have in common? They are some of the 20-plus animal species that have been cloned since the first, a tadpole, was cloned in 1952.

Would you clone a favorite pet?

And would you pay $50,000 to do so? In 2004, Julie from Texas did just that. The result? Little Nicky was produced from the DNA of Julie's beloved seventeen-year-old Maine Coon cat. Animal rights activists criticized the move, saying Julie could have used this big sum to help provide homes for thousands of stray animals instead.

Would you eat a cloneburger?

That is, a burger made from a cloned cow? What if it made it cheaper? It would cost far more to produce a single cloned cow than to breed one naturally. The first cloned calf was born in February of 1997, named Gene (get it?) and now living in the Minnesota Education Center. Other cloned cattle have been named Second Chance, 86 Squared, Betty, Cathy, and Daisy.

Would you bring back the dinosaurs?

Or, at the very least, clone an endangered animal? In 2001, scientists introduced Ombretta, a seven-month-old lamb, to the world. Ombretta was the first genetic clone of an endangered mammal to survive beyond infancy. Ombretta's ancestors, the European mouflon, originally lived in the Mediterranean islands of Cyprus, Corsica, and Sardinia and nearly died out over one hundred years ago.

Would you accept a pig kidney?

What if it could save your life? For over a decade, scientists have been on a quest to create organs for transplant from pigs into humans. A set of five piglet clones, born in 2000, and named Millie, Christa, Alexis, Carrel, and Dotcom, were an important first step in this process.

CLONED ANIMALS

carp	gaur	rabbit
cat	goat	rat
cattle	horse	rhesus monkey
deer	mice	sheep
dog	mouflon	water buffalo
ferret	mule	wolf
frog (tadpole)	pig	
fruit flies	Pyrenean ibex	

Monsters of Matter and Mind

Komodo dragon, sea serpent, oarfish,
Loch Ness monster, Tasmanian devil . . .
some of these monsters are real, some are not.
Learn the facts so you are not fooled by fiction.

KOMODO DRAGON

These meat-eating lizards live underground
in New York subways.

FICTION! Three to five thousand Komodo dragons live in the harsh climate of the Indonesian islands of Flores, Gila Montang, Rinca, and Komodo.

Baby Komodos start off eating insects and small lizards, but full-grown adults could eat a human.

FACT! Komodo dragons will eat almost anything, including bird eggs, deer, goats, wild pigs, smaller dragons, large water buffalo, and even humans—sometimes digging up shallow graves to do so!

This largest living species of lizard can weigh
as much as a lion.

FACT! Though they usually weigh about 150 pounds, the largest Komodo on record is ten feet long and weighs 370 pounds. Lions typically weigh between 265 and 420 pounds. An American crocodile can weigh up to 2,000 pounds.

LOCH NESS MONSTER

The Loch Ness monster is named for the gigantic Scottish lake it is rumored to live in.

FACT! *Loch* is the Irish and Scottish Gaelic term for a lake or sea inlet. The deepest point of this freshwater loch is 755 feet—deep enough to cover a building 50 stories tall!

The most famous picture of Nessie (an affectionate nickname for the cryptid) was taken in 1934 but was revealed as a hoax in 1994.

FACT! It is widely believed that the photo of the supposedly twenty-five-foot-long creature was actually of a three-foot-long toy submarine with a sculpted head attached.

Scientists have studied the Loch Ness monster's skeleton to prove its existence.

FICTION! Otters, fish, and every other animal that lives in the loch leave behind physical signs of their existence: footprints, signs of feeding, and eventually, a skeleton. Because there are no physical signs of Nessie, scientists doubt she exists.

TASMANIAN DEVIL

This twenty-pound marsupial's fuzzy ears turn bright red when threatened or excited.

FACT! In addition, a tassie will let out a bloodcurdling screech, point its tail straight up in the air, and stamp its feet during a battle over food or territory. Devils do NOT like to share. They are so fierce they often take on prey more than twice their own size.

Sarcophilus harrisii, *the scientific name for Tasmanian devil, means "Harris's meat lover."*

FACT! These ferocious devils eat carrion (rotting meat) geese, chickens, small farm animals, lizards, insects, seeds, fruits, and have a particular fondness for wombats. They enjoy every part of their prey, including hair and bones.

Tasmanian devils spin in fast circles and move across the land like a tornado.

FICTION! This idea comes from the cartoon devil named Taz. In reality, devils are not known for their speed; the fastest they can move is about fifteen miles an hour for about one mile. Instead, they are to be feared for their powerful jaws that can open nearly eighty degrees wide!

Creepy Candle

When you can't get your hands on a pumpkin, make a spooky lantern out of a green pepper.

You'll need:

 1 large green pepper

 1 sharp paring knife

 1 cutting board

 1 spoon—the serrated edges of a grapefruit spoon will come in handy, but a cereal spoon is fine.

 1 black marker

 1 tealight candle

 1 box of matches

 2 tablespoons of your favorite salad dressing

Proceed:

1 With an adult's help, carefully cut around the stem at the top of the pepper. This hole should be just large enough to fit a spoon through. Set aside stem and all other pepper clippings.

2 Use the spoon to scrape out the seeds and the white parts from the inside of the pepper. If necessary, scrape the bottom of the pepper to make a flat surface for the candle.

3 Draw a creepy face on one side of the pepper, the more ghastly the better! Give your nightmarish night-light unique features, like hairy eyebrows, sharp fangs, a strange nose, or lopsided ears. With an adult's help, use the knife to carve out your face shapes. Set aside the pepper clippings.

4 With a parent's help, light the candle and place it inside.

5 Dim the lights, dip the pepper clippings in salad dressing, and enjoy the ghoulish light!

NOTE: Ask an adult for help with this craft and any craft that calls for a sharp objects or fire. An adult who can reattach sliced-off fingers and work a fire extinguisher is especially useful!

VARIATIONS

- Use different types of novelty candles for a variety of effects. Trick candles and those with a sparkling wick add an extra element of surprise.

- Use red, yellow, or orange peppers for a different sort of ghoulish look.

- Get several peppers and instead of a face, cut out a letter on each pepper to spell a spooky word, like *Boo!*

The Good, the Bad, and the Ugly

Just because you don't see plants pretending to be your dad doesn't mean there's not a whole lot of freaky flowers out there. And while none of these will tie you up, some of them will assault your senses.

THE GOOD

ALOE VERA

If you've ever had a bad case of sunburn, you have paid thankful homage to the aloe vera plant, as its internal gel is used to soothe minor burns and skin rashes. You can find skin products that contain aloe at most grocery stores, or grow your own. Simply snip the succulent leaves and squeeze the cooling gel onto your skin. Ahhhhhh.

PEPPERMINT

In addition to its pleasing smell and yummy flavor, peppermint is useful for a variety of ailments. People have used this green herb to help them fall asleep, remember things, soothe a hacking cough, settle an upset stomach, and, of course, make their breath smell better! It's easy to grow, and people have been doing so for ten thousand years.

THE BAD

PITCHER PLANT

This carnivorous plant is usually bad news only if you are an insect, but larger varieties of this plant have eaten prey as large as a rat! The sneaky plant attracts curious insects with its brightly colored rim and a nectar-filled, pitcher-shaped bulb. Insects come to take a quick sip and slide down the rim to be trapped forever! Other meat-eating plants include the Venus flytrap, the Cape sundew, and the Titan butterwort.

HEMLOCK

Helpful plants like the aloe vera and peppermint may convince you that you can wander up to anything you find in the forest and use it to help you feel better. But you shouldn't eat any old plant you find without knowing the facts first. With its lacy leaves and pretty white flowers, hemlock looks innocent enough, but ingesting as few as six to eight fresh leaves could kill you. In fact, in ancient Greece, hemlock was used to poison condemned prisoners.

THE UGLY

CORPSE PLANT or DEVIL'S TONGUE

This strange plant has the notoriety of being both revolting to look at AND to smell. When it blooms, which perhaps thankfully is only once every four to six years for about three days, it stinks of rotten meat, a smell that attracts a carrion-eating beetle. That's right, a beetle that eats rotting meat. If your nose has a hankering for other plants that smell like a dozen rotten eggs, a dead hippo, or, say, an outhouse in August, check out the Drakaea glyptodon orchid, dragon arum, or Rafflesia arnoldii.

CORPSE FLOWER

Next time you're hoofing it through the rain forests of Malaysia, keep your eyes—and nose—peeled for this olfactory monstrosity. With a smell like decaying flesh and a red and spotty surface that would rival a zitty teenager, this rare plant is hard to miss. Swarms of flies like to cluster around the three-foot-wide flower—the largest in the world. Unlike other plants, this parasitic creation has no leaves, stems, or roots. Weird!

"YOWWWWWWWWW!"

That's me, Jack Harmon, screaming my head off. I was on the school bus, heading home, howling in pain. As usual.

You would scream too if Mick Owens had you in an armlock. Mick shoved my arm up behind me till I heard my bones and muscles snap and pop.

"YOWWWWWWW!" I repeated.

Nothing new here. Big Mick and his friend Darryl "The Hammer" Oliva like to beat me up, tease me, and torture me on the bus every afternoon.

Last week, our sixth-grade English teacher, Miss Harris, had a long, serious talk in class about bullying. I guess Mick and Darryl were out that day.

Otherwise, they would know that bullying is bad.

Why do they do it? Because I'm smaller than

them? Because I'm a skinny little guy who looks like a third-grader? Because I scream easily?

No.

These two super-hulks like to get up in my face because it's FUN.

They think it's funny. It makes them laugh. You should see the big grins on their faces whenever I beg and plead for them to pick on someone their own size.

And then, as soon as I start to scream, it's belly-laugh time for those two losers.

One day, I complained to Charlene, the school bus driver. But she said, "I'm a bus driver — not a referee."

Not too helpful.

And so here we were in the narrow aisle at the back of the bus. Mick with a big grin on his red, round-cheeked face. Me with my arm twisted behind my back.

Darryl watched from his seat. The other kids on the bus faced forward, pretending nothing was happening.

"YOWWWWWWW!"

Mick swiped his big fist at my head — and tugged off my Red Sox cap.

"Hey — give it back!" I cried. I made a grab for it. But he sent it sailing across the aisle to Darryl.

Darryl caught it and waved it at me. "Nice cap, dude."

I dove for it. Stumbled and fell halfway down the aisle. Darryl passed my cap back to his good buddy.

I turned, breathing hard. "Give it back."

"It's MY cap now," Mick said. He slapped it onto his curly blond hair. His head is so big, the cap didn't fit.

I dove again, hands outstretched. I almost grabbed the cap back, but Mick heaved it to Darryl. I swung around to Darryl, and he tossed it over my head back to Mick.

The bus slowed, then bumped to a stop. I bounced hard into the back of my seat. I glanced out the window. We were at Mick's house.

"Give me my Red Sox cap," I said. I stuck out my hand.

"You want it?" Mick grinned at me. "You really want it? Here."

He held the cap upside down in front of him and spit into it. A big white sticky glob.

"Here," he said. "You still want it?"

I stared into the cap. Stared at the disgusting white glob of spit.

Darryl hee-hawed like a donkey. He thinks everything Mick does is a riot.

"You still want your cap?" Mick repeated. He held it out of my reach. "Tell you what, Jacko. Give me your watch and you can have your cap."

"That's totally fair," Darryl said.

"No way!" I cried. "My grandfather gave me this watch. No way!"

The watch was a special present for my twelfth birthday. It means a lot to me. I never take it off.

"How about it, Jacko?" Mick stuck his hand out. "The watch for your Red Sox cap."

"Yo, Mick. See your house outside the window?" Charlene yelled from behind the wheel. "You want to keep us all here till dinnertime? What's your mom serving us?"

A few kids laughed at that. But most kids are too terrified of Mick to ever laugh around him.

"Mick, stop torturing Jack," Charlene yelled. "Give him back his cap and get off my bus!"

"Okay, okay. No problem," Mick said with a sneer.

He jammed the cap onto my head, so hard my feet nearly went through the bus floor. I could feel the sticky glob of spit in my hair.

Mick trotted to the door at the front. Darryl gave me a friendly punch in the ribs. Then he followed his buddy off the bus.

I let out a long sigh of relief. I had survived another trip home on the school bus. I watched Mick and Darryl jog up the driveway to Mick's little redbrick house. They punched each other as they ran. You know. Kidding around.

I slumped into the nearest seat. I shut my eyes and took a deep breath.

No permanent wounds. That meant it was a good day.

Glancing down, I saw something on the seat next to me. A silvery cell phone.

I hesitated for a moment, just staring at it. Then I reached over and picked up the phone.

And that's when the nightmare began.

2

The school bus jerked to another stop. I nearly dropped the phone.

A blond-haired girl jumped off. She waved to a friend on the bus.

I glanced down the aisle. Only two kids and me still on the bus. My house is always the next-to-last stop because I live near the border of our town.

I raised the phone and studied it. It was one of those really thin smartphones. It had a big, black screen. The phone felt cool and sleek in my hand.

I found the POWER button on the top and pushed it. A few seconds later, the screen lit up, bright blue. Then the screen filled with icons. Dozens of them. All kinds of apps.

The phone was *loaded*.

I flipped through the screens of icons. There were games, and magazines, and news, and sports.

I studied them for a while. Then I raised the phone to my ear.

I didn't expect to hear anything. So the girl's voice made me jump.

"Hi, Jack," she said. She half-talked, half-whispered. "Don't scream. I've been waiting for you. I'm your new friend."

"Huh?"

I lowered the phone and stared at it. The screen had gone blank. Solid gray. No icons.

I pressed the phone to my ear. "Who *is* this?" I asked.

"It's me, your new friend." Her voice was soft and whispery.

I thought hard. I struggled to figure out who it could be.

"Mindy? Is that you?" I said finally.

Mindy is my little sister Rachel's babysitter. She comes to our house after school every afternoon and stays till Mom and Dad get home.

Mindy is a real joker. She likes to play all kinds of tricks on me. Rachel always thinks it's a riot.

I spoke into the phone. "This is one of your dumb jokes — *isn't* it, Mindy."

"It's no joke," the girl replied. "Don't you want to be my new friend?"

"You sure you're not Mindy?" I said. "You sound a lot like Mindy."

"I don't know Mindy," the girl whispered. "I only know you. You're my only friend, Jack."

"Whoa. Wait," I said.

It couldn't be Mindy, I told myself. *How could*

Mindy know I would pick up this phone? How could Mindy know the number?

My mind was spinning. "I . . . think you have the wrong number," I said finally. "This isn't my phone, and —"

I heard her sigh. "If it's the wrong number, how do I know your name?" she breathed.

"Well . . . Come on. So it *is* Mindy!" I said. "Ha-ha. I'm laughing. But enough — okay?"

"I'm *not* Mindy," the girl snapped. Her voice was suddenly sharp and cold. "Don't make me angry," she said. "Whatever you do, Jack, don't make me angry."

Catch the MOST WANTED Goosebumps® villains UNDEAD OR ALIVE!

NOW A MAJOR
MOTION PICTURE
JACK BLACK
Goosebumps
VILLAGE ROADSHOW PICTURES
THIS FILM IS NOT YET RATED. FOR FUTURE INFO GO TO FILMRATINGS.COM
/GoosebumpsTheMovie
SCHOLASTIC
COLUMBIA PICTURES
a Sony Company